BACK HOME

The Williamson Papers #3

TOM WILLIAMS

Published by Accent Press Ltd 2016

ISBN 9781783756445

PREFACE

This is the third account of John Williamson's life. It was sent to me by the same anonymous donor as the second. I had not expected a third episode, for the Williamson who had experienced the adventures recounted in *Cawnpore* was a broken man and it seemed unlikely that his life would contain anything more of note. In fact, it seems that he was to have one final adventure, this time back in the land of his birth.

I don't know what was in Williamson's mind when he wrote this. The story of his time in Borneo (published as *The White Rajah*) was written when he was wrestling with a problem that he thought writing could help him solve. *Cawnpore* appears to have been an early draft of something he had perhaps intended one day to publish. This manuscript, though, seems to have been written simply as a record for himself, almost like an extended diary entry. Perhaps that's why much of it appears to be an attempt to justify behaviour that he clearly has doubts about and why, here and there, he seems to have been not entirely as truthful as in his other accounts. (There's a note at the end which discusses this.)

Unlike *Cawnpore*, this manuscript was not divided into chapters, but I have added these breaks in for the convenience of the modern reader. I have also corrected some spelling errors. Williamson was, by the time he wrote this, a man who expressed himself well on paper and, had he intended it for publication, I am sure he would have made these corrections himself. Otherwise I have left well alone.

Williamson does seem to be looking back on his life and there are frequent references to his time in Borneo and India. For those who haven't read *The White Rajah* or *Cawnpore*, it's probably helpful to have a brief introduction to the man and his adventures.

John Williamson was born to a family of labourers on a farm in Devon. His family died when he was a child and as soon as he was old enough he left the farm to become a seaman. As a young man he was on the crew of Sir James Brooke's vessel, the *Royalist*. He travelled to Borneo with Brooke and became his interpreter. Sir James, like Williamson, was gay and eventually a relationship developed between them. When Brooke became the ruler of Sarawak, a province in the north-west of Borneo, Williamson lived with him, ostensibly as his assistant. Brooke taught Williamson to read and write, and eventually Williamson played a significant role in the administration of the country. He was deeply in love with Brooke and shared his lover's desire to do his best for the inhabitants. However, when Brooke called in the British Navy to annihilate the pirates who preyed on his people, Williamson could not live with the consequences. Appalled by the scale of the killing, he left Brooke and travelled to India.

Arriving in India, Williamson took a job with the East India Company, as an assistant to the Collector in Cawnpore. He enjoyed the work and came to love the place and its people, even forming a relationship with one of the local Indian princelings. When the Indian Mutiny started, he found himself torn between his conflicting loyalties. As he tried to be true to both his Indian and European friends, he ended up witnessing massacres of the Europeans by the Indians and the appalling retaliation that the British inflicted after the war was over. Although he survived Cawnpore and was seen as a hero by the East India Company, he was a broken man and returned to England.

He had written accounts of his adventures in Borneo and in India and this instalment of the Williamson Papers follows on immediately from the end of *Cawnpore*, with him having just put ashore in Plymouth...

Tom Williams

CHAPTER ONE

I have got in the way of writing about the chapters that have shaped my life, and now I take up my pen again to tell the story of what I expect to be my last adventure.

In the summer of 1859, I found myself once more in England. I had put ashore in Plymouth, where I had first set out on a seafarer's life more than a quarter of a century earlier. My course, it seemed to me, had run full circle, and it felt only natural that I should walk northwards now, seeking out Mr Slattery's farm and the world of my childhood.

My time in Borneo had left me well provided for, and the East India Company was generous in its pension to a survivor of Cawnpore, but, though there was plenty of money to draw on in the bank, I had arrived ashore with little more than a change of clothes and a bag of gold for my journey. The sovereigns, it is true, gave a healthy weight to my purse and I could easily have purchased some fashionable clothes and a horse on which to travel to the village of my birth. But it was June, the sun was shining, and I welcomed the opportunity to allow myself to believe, for a few days, that I was still the same honest labourer I had been when I was last in Devon. So it was that I set out to walk. I had one pair of stout shoes and a change of clothes that I carried in a pack upon my back. I changed a couple of the sovereigns into copper and silver that would draw less attention and sewed the rest into the lining of my coat. I was, to any I met on the road, just another sailor home from the sea. Even my tan, so dark that I had been able to pass as an Indian while living in the subcontinent, was beginning to fade.

I had dreamt of England in my years away. It was not, it is true, exactly as I had remembered – or, rather, fondly imagined – it to be. After the vast landscapes of India and the huge, impenetrable jungles of Borneo, England appeared cramped, the high roads mere lanes, the lanes barely tracks across the miniature landscape. It seemed, too, almost empty of people. My memory of Plymouth was of a bustling port but now, after Calcutta, I thought it a backwater in which a few sailors and merchants were no substitute for the teeming humanity and animal excitement of that city. At the same time, those few individuals whom I saw looked as if, in the rapidity of their locomotion and the enthusiasm of their activity, they were attempting to make up in sheer force of will what they lacked in numbers. Everything in England moved so fast. Three times in my first hours ashore I was nearly ridden down, once by a coach and twice by simple farm carts, which thundered along the cobbled streets as if a minute's delay might be fatal to their drivers' plans.

Outside the town the pace of life appeared more leisurely, but even here the labourers in the fields worked with a steady rhythm that was alien to the Indians' leisurely approach to life. No beggars greeted me with their demands for alms. No Brahmins sat with their empty food bowls waiting for my donation. Indeed, when I entered a village, I would often see the constable keep a wary eye on me in case I might be an indigent who, if still in the parish as darkness fell, would need to be fed and housed overnight before I could be shuffled on to be another village's responsibility.

When I had last been in England, King William was on the throne. Sailor Bill had seemed a cheery fellow. The war with France had ended less than twenty years before and King William's reign always had something of a celebratory feel to it. Now, though, our monarch was

Queen Victoria, and England presided over the greatest Empire the world had ever seen. Even in the Devon countryside, life moved with a purpose. Every man toiling in the fields, every woman hanging out her laundry – all played their part in the business of Empire, bringing, though the labourer might not have the leisure to appreciate it, unparalleled prosperity to the nation. Here was the very mainspring of that machine that sent its armies and its missionaries across the globe, to bring civilisation and Christianity to the peoples of the world, though, in my experience, they might be ignorant of their want of either.

The sight of so much industry was at once both impressive and unnerving. I felt as if I were a mere bumpkin, plucked from some obscure backwater and suddenly at the busy heart of things, but the people that I met were civil and, when I stopped for refreshment at a tavern, the ale was good and the landlord as friendly as might be. So I carried on my journey in an uncertain frame of mind, part excited and happy to be back in England, part apprehensive at the changes that I found.

My way took me across Dartmoor, its open spaces reminding me a little of India, but it seemed an empty, desolate place. I spent the night in Moretonhampstead, finding an inn almost in the shadow of the old church tower. The church was not old, as the temples in India might be old, but since I left England I had seen no Christian churches that were many years older than me and thus, before I set off to complete my journey, I went inside and sat awhile there. I tried to pray, but no words came. So I shrugged my pack onto my shoulders and started off again across the moor.

I arrived at Mr Slattery's farm early in the afternoon. It was a fine day and the neat fields around the farmhouse were soothing to my soul after the barrenness of the moor. I was as cheerful as I had been for a while when I saw a woman cleaning the steps before the farmhouse door and hailed her.

She turned to me with a look neither welcoming nor hostile, but curious to see who might have disturbed her day, for the farm was some way from the road.

I gave her my name, but it was clear that it meant nothing to her.

'My family used to work on the farm. I was raised in the cottages at the foot of Lower Field.' She still looked puzzled. 'They died in '31. When there was sickness here.'

'Ah, that would explain it. That was ten years before I came here. Would you be looking for Mr Slattery?'

I supposed I was. It may seem strange that I had journeyed so far with so little idea of what I was to do when I reached my destination. But you must remember that I had suffered much in India and I was drawn home as a wounded animal seeks its lair. It was almost thirty years since I had last walked the path that led up to this farmhouse, but it was still as near a home as anywhere I had. Everything I loved in India had been destroyed and there was no question of my returning to Borneo. So, when I had found myself free to retire to any spot upon the globe, it had seemed inevitable that I must make my way back to Devon. And now that I was here, it made sense to call first upon Mr Slattery.

I looked at the young woman – I had not really registered how much younger than me she was – as she stood with one hand upon her hip, as if uncertain that I could have any honest business with the master of her household.

'He had our family Bible with him for safekeeping. Now that I am home, I suppose I should take charge of it again.'

It was a foolish thing to say. The Bible, I would guess, weighed as much as all my other possessions together and I had no idea what I would do with it if it were returned to me. But I had to give the woman some reply and these were the first words that blurted from my mouth. I remembered Mr Slattery in the way that a young boy would remember a man who had been like a minor deity in his parents' world. The farm, I now knew, was small, but when I was a child it was the largest farm I could imagine and Mr Slattery appeared a great personage. Even now I was grown and had travelled the world and been accounted a person of some importance, part of me still believed that Mr Slattery would be able to take my life in hand and advise me on what I should do now.

'That will be old Mr Slattery.' Her speech softened a little. 'I'm sorry. He's dead. He died ten years since.' She must have seen the look of confusion and uncertainty on my face, because she hurried to continue. 'I'm sure my husband – that's young Mr Slattery – I'm sure he can give you your Bible.'

I hesitated and she spoke again. 'You can go and see him over at Spinney Acre, if you want. They're singling the turnips up there and Mr Slattery has gone to see that the girls are doing good work.'

I well remembered singling turnips. Weeding and thinning the rows of roots was backbreaking labour, always performed by women. When I had been old enough to stay alongside my mother in the fields, I had been allowed to help. I was not trusted with a hoe, for it was skilled work and carelessness with the tool could damage the vegetables that were to be left in the ground, but children were allowed to pull weeds by hand where they grew too close to the turnips to be cleared with the hoe. I doubt that my efforts materially assisted the gang of women, but it kept me near my mother, allowing her to work and introducing me to the life that everybody expected for me, working on the farm.

I know now how hard it was for the women who stood bent over their hoes – for short handles were preferred for

5

the job, allowing more accuracy in the task. As a child, though, I had innocently thought my time in the fields to be just a game that my mother had devised for me. Though I might have grown tired and fractious after ten hours alongside her, I still had happy memories of those sunny summer days – for singling is always done in dry weather. I resolved, therefore, to make my way to Spinney Acre and see Mr Slattery there, hoping to rekindle memories of the time before my parents departed this earth.

I thanked Mrs Slattery and set off along the path that led towards the turnip field. Although I had been so many years away, once I had started walking my feet guided me almost without my thinking of the way at all. Spinney Acre was almost a mile from the farmhouse, but, less than a quarter of an hour after I had bade farewell to his wife, I was raising my hat to Mr Slattery.

He had been watching half-a-dozen women hoeing under the supervision of one man, whose mouth, twisted into a frown around a corncob pipe, suggested that he would as soon be left to supervise them alone. Slattery also did not look especially happy and he greeted me somewhat curtly. When I explained who I was, though, he welcomed me kindly enough and offered me his hand.

'I've been watching to see how the work progresses. Some of the women have been overly careless and a deal of the crop was damaged yesterday,' he explained. 'Still, I think old Ted –' he nodded towards the man with the pipe, 'will be more attentive to them now. I will stroll over to the Meadow and see how far we are from cutting the hay.'

It seemed early to me to be thinking of haymaking, but the crops were advanced for the season. I had wondered that I had not felt the chill of an English summer after my time in India, but now I supposed that it was an unusually warm year. I made some remark to this effect to Mr Slattery, and he agreed. So, in talking about the weather, we established a common bond in time-honoured fashion, and soon I was telling him some of what had befallen me since I had last walked these paths.

'You have prospered, then, while you have been away.'

I owned that I had, but wondered that it was so clear, given that I lacked the outward show of wealth.

Slattery laughed. 'There's no need to look so puzzled. It is clear to any man of discernment that your travels have been attended with success. True, your clothes are not in the latest fashion, but you are newly returned to England, so I would hardly expect them to be. But they are well made and not those of a vagabond or a common sailor. All that is secondary, though, to your manner. You introduced yourself to me as an equal and I responded automatically in the same way. Yet many an itinerant labourer importunes me in the fields and, I confess, I am inclined to dismiss them out of hand.'

My attempt to play the part of the common man had, it seemed, completely failed. I remembered the times I had walked disguised as a beggar through the streets of India and how successful my imposture had been there. Had I been so long away that I could more easily take on the manners of the Far East than fit unnoticed into the society of my own country?

The failure of my disguise had, however, proved a blessing. Mr Slattery had decided that I was a capital fellow and insisted that I join him in the farmhouse for his lunch. 'It will be simple enough fare, but you'll remember that from your youth here.'

It was true that the food that Mrs Slattery placed on the table for us was nominally the same bread and cheese that my mother had laid upon our own board, but there was little in the fresh bread and creamy cheese straight from the dairy that resembled the dried husks and hard cheddar of my youth. Nor was my mother's kitchen generally graced with butter and preserves and, though I had never been allowed to drink the cider that used to be set at my father's place, I have little doubt that Slattery's was not drawn from the same barrel. Still, I could hardly complain of hypocrisy when his sharp eye had so soon realised that I was hardly the labourer that I had hoped to appear. Slattery was a successful farmer. To my mind, it spoke in his favour that he lunched on bread and cheese, as did his workers, even if it was not the same bread, and the cheese had not come from the same dairy.

Over our meal, he quizzed me about what had brought me back to Bickleigh. Our conversation made me think rationally about my purpose, something I had put off throughout the long voyage home.

'It's difficult to say,' I admitted. 'I suppose that, having spent so long in countries that are not my own, it is natural to seek to return to the one place on earth that always must be.'

'I fear, though, that you will find it much changed.'

I shook my head at that, for surely the English countryside would prove immutable, whatever was happening in the rest of the world.

'There are fewer people here, for one thing,' he said. 'Life here is hard and men are certain that they can find a better living in the factories that are springing up in all the cities of England. We have the railway now, sir, and London is a great draw.'

It was strange to think of railways running all the way from London to Devon. Such a network of iron rails was planned for India – indeed, I had often met the engineers who had come to Cawnpore to survey the route. People had said that the railways would change the whole way of life in that country, and I had been happy to agree with them. I had never thought that the same might be true of England.

'You can travel to the capital in a day,' Slattery said. 'Leave at breakfast and be there in time for supper!'

His tone made it all too clear that he did not really

approve. 'They're even trying to change our clocks. The station clock tells the time in London and they say we should set all our clocks to that time.' He had been sipping at his cider and now he banged the glass down on the table, apparently stirred to passion by this perceived outrage. 'We are to have the clocks striking noon a quarter of an hour before the sun reaches its zenith. It's practically sacrilege, sir! The time set down by the railway is to supersede the time laid down by God.'

Mrs Slattery had obviously heard this view expressed before. She allowed herself a quiet sigh, took a cloth to mop the spilled cider, and poured more into his glass.

Slattery caught her eye and grinned, embarrassed. 'Mrs Slattery considers that I have a bee in my bonnet and I probably do. The railways are progress and progress is doubtless a wonderful thing, but it is unsettling. Men who had been content all their lives in our little village take it into their heads to move away. The Great Wen exerts an evil fascination on so many.' I looked puzzled and Mr Slattery was forced to explain that the Great Wen was what many folk had taken to calling the nation's capital, as it grew like a malignant cyst. 'But for all that many call it by foul names, its influence is almost mesmeric. I think you will find many of your old friends are no longer here.'

Again, his words gave me pause for thought. When we say that we remember home, or we wish to return to our home, it is not geography that first comes to mind. Home is defined by the people we remember and, without them, geography alone cannot relieve the pangs of homesickness. But where were the people I had grown up with? My parents were dead and the fever that had taken them had taken, also, many of those I had known as a child. Others, like the first Mr Slattery, had grown old and died while I had been away. I chewed thoughtfully on the bread and cheese while I tried to remember any of my playmates who I might see again. I had been a lonely child. Indeed, Mr Slattery had put me to work with horses because I seemed more comfortable with the farm beasts than with people. There had been one boy, though – Michael. He had been a year or two older than me, a big boy, barrel-chested even as a lad. He was strong and, though the fever struck down his family as well as mine, he had survived. He had been kind to me when I had been shunned or bullied by the other children and I had sought him out once I had decided to leave the village. I remembered his eyes, for they were a dark blue, although his hair was brown. When I last saw him, and shook his hand at parting, I am not sure that I did not see the trace of a tear in those eyes.

'Michael,' I said. I spoke almost unconsciously, but Mr Slattery replied immediately.

'Michael Radford.'

I nodded.

'It's funny you should mention him. He seemed settled enough here, but then, a few months back, he did exactly what I've just been talking about: upped and left for London. He never married, so I suppose he felt there was nothing to hold him here, but he was a good man and a useful worker and I was sorry to lose him.'

Mrs Slattery, who had taken little part in our conversation, now interrupted. 'I'm a bit worried about him. I had thought to hear some news, but there has been nothing.'

'What did you expect?' Her husband raised his eyebrows to me, inviting me to share his confident masculine belief in the foolishness of the female sex. 'I doubt he's a letter-writing man.'

'Michael has a fine hand and writes well.' She turned to me. 'I help the Reverend Soane at the Poor School and sometimes Michael would assist us, in the winter when there was less work to do about the farm.'

'My wife, Mr Williamson, is a sentimental woman.' He

said it as if it were a fault, but his smile belied his words. 'She thinks everybody is as warm and generous as herself.'

'My husband mocks me, sir, but if anybody was sentimental, it was Michael. He had a kind heart and cared for his friends here. He left only because he thought he could make a better life in town and he promised to write and let us know how he thrived there. I'm sure some ill has befallen him, or he would have sent word.'

There was a moment's silence, but then, before the conversation could grow uncomfortable, Mr Slattery said that he intended now to go to the stables, for he had a draught mare about to foal and he wanted to check on her. 'You said that you used to work with the horses, Mr Williamson. Would you care to join me?'

I was happy to agree and, thanking Mrs Slattery for the meal, I rose and followed her husband out into the farmyard.

'I think the stables are new since your time. We had a block built on the latest principles.'

I made appropriate sounds of admiration, but I was sincere in my appreciation of the building, which was larger than the one I remembered. Inside, the extra space meant more ventilation and the stench of ammonia, though still prevalent, was not as pungent as I remembered. The stalls were wider and, at the end, there was a loose box, the size of two stalls. It was in this that the mare stood placidly eating from her manger. Slattery looked at her critically. 'She's late to foal,' he said, 'but I think she looks well enough. What is your opinion?'

I had not been close to a draught horse since I left England, for oxen or buffalo are used in this role in the East, but I found I remembered well enough. I prodded at her rump and looked beneath her belly to see her teats and agreed that she should drop soon and generally appeared in good condition.

11

'I should offer you employment in my stables, I think,' Slattery said. For a moment I thought he was making me a serious offer of employment and, transported in that instant back to my youth, I might have knuckled my forehead and accepted. Then I saw the grin on his face and I was back in the present: John Williamson, late of the East India Company and in a good way to being a gentleman myself. 'Seriously, Williamson, do you have any plans? You could stay with us for a few weeks if you are determined to settle hereabouts and you could see what opportunities the countryside might offer. Perhaps you might breed horses or become a gentleman farmer and come and condescend to me from time to time because I do this for a livelihood and not for amusement.'

I remembered poor Lydia Hillersdon and her sheep that she was so proud of back in India. I had no wish to play at farming as she had, and I was too old, I thought, to start an agricultural career in earnest.

'I will not set up in competition with you, sir. I had wondered if I might not buy a house nearby and build a library where I might spend my time in contemplation and study. And, perhaps, in drinking the odd jug of claret, in which enterprise you would be welcome to join me.'

Slattery looked suitably satisfied with this plan. 'But would you not find life dull here, after such adventures as you must have had?'

I owned that it would be quiet. 'But really,' I said, 'I have had adventures enough for one lifetime.' I could not, of course, but think of Cawnpore, and the horrors I had seen there, and I think some of this must have shown in my face, for Slattery was quick to move the conversation on.

'If you're looking to settle down in comfort, maybe you should think of buying The Grange.'

The suggestion shocked me. The Grange was the largest house in the village, if you excluded the castle, which was a barely habitable ruin. The idea that someone like me might buy The Grange seemed a subversion of the natural order but, as I allowed myself to even consider the possibility, I realised that I had more than enough money to do so.

'Is it on the market?'

'Has been since old Hodge died. His widow has not the money to keep it up and would as soon move into Plymouth where her daughter is married to someone in business at the port.'

Could I buy The Grange? I remembered Mr Hodge. He had seemed, to us children, the epitome of a rich gentleman. We took care to stay out of his way, for if people of that class took against you, things would go badly indeed. If he rode past us as we walked along the lane, we would stand respectfully to one side, doffing our caps and looking downward with a sort of half-bow. Was I now of the same class as Mr Hodge? My wealth had, up to now, been just some notional thing and, indeed, in London it would be accounted a very small fortune but here, in Devon, it would let me live high on the hog for the rest of my days.

I resolved to think seriously about buying The Grange, or some similar property, and I accepted Mr Slattery's generous offer to stay with him at the farm, but I resolved that I should take myself away from Devon before I made any final decision. I did not want to decide the shape of the rest of my life based on what might just be a sentimental whim. I would have a look round The Grange and, if I decided it would suit me, I would appoint a man of business to explore the possibilities of purchasing it. Meanwhile, though, I would take a holiday. What point was there, after all, in being a man of means if I could not indulge myself? I would take advantage of this wonderful new railway and travel up to London. It was, after all, now the capital of a mighty empire and accounted one of the wonders of the modern world. It should surely repay a visit.

When I announced my plans over dinner a couple of days later, both Mr and Mrs Slattery seemed to approve. 'I'll find out where Michael Radford was supposed to be going,' Mrs Slattery said. 'If you're going to London, you could see if you can find him and let me know that he's all right.'

And that is how it began.

CHAPTER TWO

I bought a second-class ticket to London. Walking the roads of Devon with a pack on my back reminded me of my youth and had been a romantic gesture in its way. There would be nothing romantic, though, about seven hours in an open railway carriage. I might still not feel comfortable with the idea that I was now, as far as the acquaintances of my youth were concerned, a gentleman, but, while I would not go so far as to travel in the first-class accommodation, I was not so quixotic as to use the third.

Mr Slattery had a cart travelling up to Plymouth to carry vegetables to a grocer's store that he supplied there – 'It's a long way, but prices in the town are good and he pays a premium for my carrots this early in the season,' he said. I was to travel up on the cart. Mr Slattery would happily have given me the use of a horse, but, as I did not intend to return for some time, this was hardly practical. I would arrive too late for the train, but I would spend the afternoon in town equipping myself with appropriate clothing for a trip to the capital and then, after a night at an inn, I would be ready to set off the next morning. 'You will have no trouble finding accommodation,' Slattery assured me. 'There is such a growth of business, with the new railway, that the inns are all making more rooms available and there is talk of building an hotel.'

I was not that reassured for, if there was such a clear demand, then surely all the places might be taken. But, in the event, Slattery proved right. With my new respectability and gold coin in my purse, I secured a room with no difficulty and spent the afternoon buying myself a new wardrobe and luggage in which to carry it.

I shall say little of my journey up to London. So many people have written of the wonders of the new steam trains that it is scarcely worth my while adding to their number. It was, indeed, a remarkable experience to be carried at such speed and yet in greater comfort than had I taken a coach that travelled with but a fraction of the velocity. The countryside moved by so fast that it seemed at first quite dizzying, but I found I soon accustomed myself to it and whiled away the hours watching the workers in their fields, most of whom looked up to admire the progress of the locomotive as it passed by. I did once experiment with opening the window, but the great rush of air and the specks of soot that were carried the length of the train from the smokestack of our engine both discouraged me from repeating the experience.

I had been concerned that I might want for refreshment on the journey and I had taken the precaution of wrapping a small parcel of bread and cheese. This sat on top of my new clothes in my travelling bag, but, in the event, it proved unnecessary. The train made brief stops at the most important stations on the route – I recall Yeovil and Salisbury, where I caught a glimpse of the great Cathedral spire – and at these places the platforms were busy with men selling all sorts of food and drink for the refreshment of us weary travellers. I was able to feast on a passable hot pie washed down with honest English ale.

The locomotive and the track on which it ran were both impressive and the stations were fitting monuments to this new age of steam. But the stations I had passed through, imposing as they were, still failed to prepare me for my arrival in London. Exactly to the minute, our locomotive pulled into the terminal station at Paddington, a veritable temple to the new technology. Though smoke and steam billowed above us, still the great metal ribs of the glass ceiling could be seen arching across the sky. It was just late afternoon, the journey having taken us less than six hours.

I made my way down the platform. It was, of course, busy with all my fellow passengers, but this was nothing to the scene that met my eyes as I left the station and made my way onto the street.

It is a commonplace for old India hands to speak of the mass of humanity that throngs its cities. Certainly, the sheer number of human beings that one sees in a place like Calcutta felt infinitely greater than I could observe walking about Eastbourne Terrace. The Indian throng, though, spreads itself across the landscape, cheerfully indifferent as to pavements or thoroughfares with many individuals quietly resting, or even asleep, in a doorway or under a tree. The people I saw here moved with order and purpose, which gave the impression that the pavements were packed with a vital energy that I had never observed before. The city had grown in the time that I had been away and, in any case, my business had never taken me beyond the docks. Here in Paddington, a continual stream of men, most in top hats and almost all in dark clothing, passed in and out of the station entrances. An occasional gentleman wore the green of the militia that had been raised against the threat of a French invasion – a threat that I had not realised was being taken seriously outside the pages of the more excitable newspapers. It had been the subject of some discussion with Mr Slattery, who shared my opinion that the French could not really be expected to attack England scarcely forty years after their humiliation at Waterloo. 'They may choose another man named Napoleon as their emperor,' Slattery had opined, as his wife sighed and refilled his glass, 'but they will not dare threaten John Bull again.' We had mocked the notices calling for volunteer riflemen that had appeared prominently displayed on official notice boards in Devon, but the presence of these green coats showed that, here in the capital, there were those who believed in the possibility. Certainly, it seemed to suit the government to encourage these concerns, for I had already seen a recruiting poster for the militia displayed at the station to be read as soon as passengers arrived in London. The uniforms proved that there were already men who had answered the call, though their dull green made little impression on the generally monochrome appearance of the crowd. This was relieved only by the occasional female figure, whose clothing brought flashes of colour – all the more conspicuous because these figures commanded a few inches of empty space, as their wide skirts demanded more of the street and the natural chivalry of the gentleman around them added a respectable cordon of clear pavement. Otherwise the roadside seemed completely occupied with as many humans as could be fitted on it. A glance at the road beyond, though, and the pavement suddenly seemed, by contrast, to offer the emptiness that one associates with tales of the Russian steppes, for the carriageway was filled with carts, carriages, hackney cabs, and every sort of conveyance that the modern world has put on the highway. An omnibus seemed marooned majestically in the centre of the thoroughfare, the advertisement panel on its side exhorting us all to purchase Oakey's Polish. It seemed impossible that any of the vehicles in this solid phalanx of traffic would be able to make any progress at all, but, as I watched, the omnibus edged a few yards eastward while, with much shouting and cursing, a drayman manoeuvred his horses into an almost imperceptible gap and thus pulled his cart a little to the West.

I had no definite plans. It is true that I had told Mrs Slattery that I would look out for Michael Radford, but she had been able to give me no clue as to where he might be. 'I was sure he would have written, or said something to the parson, but there is nothing,' she had admitted, and gone on, like the good woman she was, to insist that I not trouble myself about it on her account. Certainly a search for Michael Radford was no justification for the visit, though I had told her that I would make such inquiries as I could. In truth, there was no real reason for my visit at all. I had simply decided to enjoy my leisure and relative affluence by spending a few days in the capital. Now, faced with the reality of the size of the city, I knew just two things: firstly, that finding Radford would be no easy task and, secondly, that I needed a room out of this bustle so that I could prepare myself for the reality of life in modern London.

The second of these objectives, at least, was easily achieved. Signs around the station pointed to Great Western's Royal Hotel which had been incorporated into Mr Brunel's plans for his terminus. I followed the arrows and, a few minutes later, I was out of the maelstrom and settled in the luxury and quiet of my own room.

I now turned my mind to Mrs Slattery's errand. How to start tracking down Michael Radford? I knew only that he had left Bickleigh the previous November. It was a sensible time to leave, because the winter brings hard times, the labourers being laid off when there is no work on the farm, and harsh weather. He had spoken of finding work in London, but he seemed to have no plans beyond that. When I had taken a drink with the other farm hands, though, there was talk that he had hoped to meet up with a younger man, one Harry Price. Harry had left for London the previous year and apparently had fallen into difficulties there. Word of this had got back to Michael through one of the guards who escorted the cider barrels up to town. It seems young Harry was taken up by the police trying to board a Plymouth train without a ticket. This had bothered Michael, who swore that Harry was an honest lad who would never have done such a thing had he the money to pay. Michael was generally known to have been close to Harry, so when he, in his turn, announced that he was leaving for the capital, there were more than a few who thought that he would likely try to find his friend.

It seemed to me that, if I wanted to find Michael, I should start by trying to trace Harry. Whether or not I found the younger man was immaterial – just by following his trail, I hoped I would be following Michael's as well.

Given that I was already at the spot where Harry had last been reported, and where Michael's quest must presumably have begun, I thought I might as well start on this immediately. There were, it is true, museums to visit, sights to see and theatrical performances to enjoy, but after only a few minutes on the London street I was already exhausted, and I resolved not to venture far from the hotel until I had had the benefit of a good night's sleep. The offices of the Great Western Railway, though, were but a few yards away so, after a refreshing cup of tea in the hotel lounge, I made my way into the station and proceeded to enquire for the manager.

I had, if I am honest, no great expectation of success. The arrest of a man for failing to pay his fare almost a year previously must surely have been forgotten by now. It seems, though, that, while human memory is fallible, the records of the Great Western Railway will remember every incident in the working of that wondrous institution until the Crack of Doom. The manager escorted me to the offices of the railway's own Police Force, where they referred to a great ledger book detailing every offence that had been committed at Paddington since the station was opened. London being a well-ordered city and the inhabitants, on the whole, less inclined to criminality than those of Calcutta, there were not so many persons charged with evading their fares as to make the search for this one individual a matter of any great difficulty. Indeed, only a few minutes seemed to have passed before the sergeant at the station desk was able to point a fat forefinger at an entry from almost a year earlier.

'Harry Price. We handed him over to the Peelers at Marylebone.'

I thanked him, offering him a small gratuity for his efforts. This was refused with a show of indignation, which may have reflected the new standards that the government claims to have brought to policing in the metropolis, or may simply have been that the manager was still within earshot.

Marylebone police station, it turned out, was almost a mile and a half away towards the West End. Uncertain of the way, and having promised myself a night's sleep before venturing into the fray of London's pavements, I decided to pursue this trail the next day.

The next morning – it was a Wednesday – dawned bright and sunny. I took myself to the station bookshop, where I purchased one of the useful maps that have become so popular with visitors to London since the Great Exhibition brought so many strangers to the city. I was relieved to have such a guide, for I do not know how I would have found Marylebone Lane without it.

The word 'Lane' suggests a minor byway in an area of rural tranquillity. This may indeed have been the case a hundred years ago, but the area to the North of Oxford Street has, since the time of King George, become a favourite resort for the upper echelons of Society and the place is now a succession of elegant squares linked by streets full of fine buildings. As it is a residential district, there were far fewer people on the street than had been the case around Paddington station, and it offered a pleasant walk. Most of the roads, being relatively newly laid out, were broad and straight, but Marylebone Lane was, as the name suggested, a narrow and meandering thoroughfare that ran more or less North to South across Wigmore Street.

21

It took some time for me to find the police station, as I had chosen to turn North, that being more towards Paddington, while the station was, in fact, to the South. Eventually, though, I discovered my error and, retracing my steps, I was soon standing beneath the reassuring blue lamp of the station house.

Again, I found the records kept by the police office were meticulous. As I now had the date of the incident, the desk sergeant was able to look it up immediately.

''Arry Price. 'Ere we are. Attempting to travel on a railway without having previously paid his fare, and with intent to avoid payment thereof. The Police Court fined him ten shillings, but there was no way he would ever find the money to pay. We kept him in the cells here for a week and then turfed 'im out.'

'Did he have an address?'

The sergeant laughed. 'If you can call it that. Queen Street.' He laughed again, then, apparently in response to the puzzlement on my face, he added, 'It's in Seven Dials.'

'Seven Dials?' I was vaguely aware of the name and had some notion that it was an area best avoided, but beyond that, I had no knowledge of it at all.

'It's a rookery.'

My expression must, again, have revealed my ignorance.

'I suppose there's no reason why a gentleman like yourself should know the rookeries, sir,' he said, kindly, if condescendingly. 'You're new to London?'

I admitted that I was.

'Well, sir, all I can say to you about the rookeries is that you are best avoiding them. Dens of vice and iniquity, sir.'

I did not feel that he was going to give me any further information, so I left the police station and returned, thoughtfully, to my hotel.

Perusal of the street plan that I had bought showed

Seven Dials to be situated just North of Covent Garden, no distance from the British Museum. Surely it could not be such a terrible place? Perhaps I could visit the Museum in the afternoon and combine it with a call on Queen Street?

I mulled over the idea, and could see no fault with the plan. However, the police sergeant's advice had been so insistent that I thought it would be wise to check with the concierge as to whether or not such a visit would be prudent. His reaction was so violent as to surprise me.

'Seven Dials, sir! You don't be wanting to be visiting there.' The concierge had, up to that point, spoken in the mellifluous tones of a gentleman's gentleman and the relapse in his grammar was the clearest indication of how seriously he viewed my proposed folly.

I felt safer pursuing the subject with a hotel employee than I had with a policeman, so I enquired about what it was that made Seven Dials such a notorious neighbourhood. It was obviously a subject that made him uncomfortable, but a few coins passed from my hand to his and, eventually, he explained something of the nature of the locality.

I had already remarked, as I walked towards Marylebone Lane, on the splendid buildings that lined my route. The concierge now explained to me that as the better classes of society had moved westward into these spacious new residences, the houses more adjacent to the city had, over time, become more or less abandoned. Nature, we are told, abhors a vacuum, and in a crowded metropolis like London any empty space is soon taken up by some of the thousands of indigents who would otherwise be sleeping on the streets. Having no legal titles to the properties, and paying no rent, they packed themselves in, scores of people living in what had once been a single dwelling. At first, the owners might have made occasional attempts to repossess their properties, or collect rent from those living there, but the new residents were many and the landlords' agents were few. Eventually the area was given over to the incomers. The rich, after all, saw no value to the properties that might justify the trouble and expense of trying to regain them and the poor, it seemed, were prepared to organise and fight for their homes. Occasional forays had been made by the police but, as the concierge explained to me, 'There's no love lost between the working man and the Peelers and it would take every policeman in London to battle their way into Seven Dials now.'

It seemed to me that he must be exaggerating. Surely lawlessness on such a scale would spill out into the respectable areas surrounding this so-called 'rookery'?

'Well, of course, it does up to a point. You'd best be careful of your watch and your pocketbook if you go to visit the Museum, sir. But the police patrol those areas in numbers and the knavery is mostly checked at the boundaries.'

As can be imagined, all these warnings gave me food for thought. I decided that I would visit the Museum and take the opportunity to have a look at the fringes of this famous rookery. I had, after all, promised Mrs Slattery that I would make enquiries after Michael Radford and it would cost me nothing to go to see the place. Just to look at it did not commit me to anything further.

I lunched at the hotel upon half a roast chicken – not an extravagance, the chicken being very small indeed – a large slice of warm ham, and some new potatoes. Thus fortified, I set off for the British Museum.

The Museum is rather further from the station hotel than is Marylebone Lane, so I resolved not to walk there. The sight of the omnibus moving so slowly through the press of traffic when I first arrived discouraged me from experimenting with that as a means of transportation, so, on the advice of the concierge, I engaged a cabriolet at the cab-stand conveniently adjacent to the station. In this contraption I bumped and rattled along the paving, scarcely any faster than the omnibus at first, but picking up speed once we were clear of the traffic. It was scarcely luxury, but it was not unpleasant, and I certainly preferred it to the palanquins in which I had been carried around Calcutta.

I will not dwell on the wonders of the Museum. The collection of objects from throughout the Empire and beyond is all too well-known. Like almost everybody visiting for the first time, I spent hours admiring the mummy cases from ancient Egypt, but I made sure to take time to enjoy the collection of animals and birds from India. Though my time in that country had been marked by great sorrow, still there were pleasant memories as well, and, though some of the animals looked dusty and, dare I say, moth-eaten in their glass cases, still they reminded me of the Nana Sahib's private zoo and my time there with Mungo Buksh.

I lingered looking at that shabby tiger and its fellows until the voice of the attendant clearing the galleries brought me to myself and I realised that it was almost seven o'clock.

Outside, the sun still shone brightly. It was warm and pleasant, and I stood for a few minutes on the Museum steps, looking at the crowd moving away as the building closed to the public. The street was busy, but it had a more relaxed air. The crowd seemed made up mainly of visitors to the metropolis, gentlemen of leisure who had been perusing the library in the Round Reading Room, and families whose children, under the careful eyes of governesses, were being brought up to town to improve their minds. Here and there, the green uniforms of the militia mingled with the crowds, for it was a fine and patriotic thing to have joined up and people were anxious that their martial ardour should not go unrecognised. It was, though, a peaceful scene. Even the militia did not, I think, really expect that the French would invade, the latest in a line of Napoleons being much exercised in fighting in Italy. It was difficult, surrounded by such palpable evidence of civilised security, to believe that across Great Russell Street, and barely half a mile away, was an area that I had twice been assured was utterly beyond the law.

My map showed that Museum Street ran South to Oxford Street. Oxford Street was one of the great thoroughfares of the new London: walking there must surely be without risk. I strolled southwards. I noticed many of those who had left the museum with me took the same course.

Museum Street turned out to be a pleasant enough little road. There were bookshops to appeal to serious students visiting the Museum and other shops offered curios for the less scholastically inclined. Museum Street runs past Oxford Street and I continued along it. Costermongers – who were, I imagined, moved on in the immediate vicinity of the Museum – had their carts upon the pavements and were selling penny pies or, for those with a sweeter tooth, cakes and tarts, or a variety of sweets. A governess who had been foolish enough to allow her charges within sight of a barrow, where jars of sweets were temptingly displayed, was insisting that they should move on without delay, while the children remonstrated with shrill voices which, I expected, would be silenced only once those desirable comestibles had been purchased. One of these street merchants, in respect to the academic nature of his potential audience, was selling old books and almanacs, though these publications were interspersed with pamphlets giving accounts of some recent hangings.

The noise and bustle created by these various tradesmen meant that I did not at first observe that there were fewer pedestrians abroad, but, in any case, the street seemed safe enough. The sun continued to shine and all seemed well with the world. The stories about Seven Dials, I decided, were no more than that. A place gets a bad reputation and myths grow up around it. There was no reason why I could not visit Queen Street. I turned right on Broad Street and continued towards the infamous rookery.

Broad Street may once have been a respectable enough road, but most of the commerce had moved North to Oxford Street. The pavements now were suddenly quieter. There were no barrows here, for few of those I saw hurrying along in worn suits and shabby hats looked likely to buy even the most tattered of second-hand books. I suddenly felt conspicuous in my smart new clothes and conscious of the gold in my purse. Was it my imagination or did some of the men loitering in doorways look at me with a calculating glance, as if weighing up the profit that they might make if they were to assault me in the street?

I told myself that I was being foolish and simply responding to the stories I had heard, but, as I approached the end of Broad Street, it was clear that I was coming to the boundaries of the civilised London I had known. The division was surprisingly sharp. To my right, the buildings were, it is true, shabby, but they bore an air of honest poverty. To my left, though, I could see the entrance to a slum such as one might have found in the most notorious reaches of Calcutta.

I suppose the first thing to remark was the stench. The density of humanity crammed together in London means that there is inevitably some olfactory evidence of the crowds of people inhabiting every street. Unfortunately, the development of a system for the removal of effluvia below ground has not kept pace with building work at street level and above. For anyone who has spent time in the East, the sanitary arrangements in London seem remarkably civilised, although the great men of the city are always demanding that 'something should be done' to improve things. At Seven Dials, however, matters had reached a completely different level. As the landlords had abandoned their properties, it seems likely that there were no arrangements for sewerage at all. Even where I stood, I could see, looking at the roads to my left, that the streets themselves were being used to carry human waste away from the buildings. I have remarked on it being an unusually warm summer. Presumably cold, wet weather brought its own problems, but it's certain that dry, warm days accentuated the foul smell wafting from this slum. The broken windows and battered doors – some seemingly no longer attached to their frames – provided visual confirmation of what my nose had already told me. These were no longer houses or homes – they were mere hovels in which the dregs of society subsisted.

That people did subsist there was all too obvious. At the end of the road where I was standing, there was hardly anyone about, but looking down towards the centre of the rookery I saw, it seemed, hundreds of figures. Many were huddled on the pavement, apparently oblivious of the filth around them. Some were lying – whether sleeping or dead I had no idea – while children skipped over their bodies as they ran in and out of the doorways. I cannot say what it was about those children that repelled me. It should have been a sight of happy innocence – I could even hear occasional laughter – but there was something about the way they moved that was utterly malevolent.

I do not know how long I stood looking down that street. I think that my sudden exposure to the reality of Seven Dials was so overwhelming that I could not think sensibly for a while. Certainly there was no question now of my visiting Queen Street that afternoon.

I was suddenly aware of somebody approaching me. I was by now so nervous that I turned on my heel ready to strike out to defend myself. Just in time, I recognised the reassuring uniform of a Metropolitan policeman.

'You weren't thinking of going down there, were you?' He nodded his head in the direction I had been staring.

I assured him that I was not.

'Best be off than,' he said. His attitude did not seem unkindly. He nodded his head again, this time in the direction of George Street, which ran North. 'I'd head up that way, sir, if I were you.'

I mumbled my thanks and set off back towards Oxford Street and civilisation.

CHAPTER THREE

My first thought was to forget about Harry Price. I just wanted to put Seven Dials out of my mind. It was a foul place, some sort of survival from a previous age. It had no business in modern London and people like me had no business in it.

Then I thought of Michael Radford. If he had, indeed, been following Harry Price, then he had presumably visited Queen Street. Where had he gone after that? Was there any chance that he was still there?

The idea of my childhood friend living – surviving, rather – in that awful place was almost too much to bear. Could I really just turn my back on him? I had, after all, promised Mrs Slattery that I would try to find him. I hesitated, but decided that it was my duty, at the least, to pay one visit to Queen Street and make some attempt to find Harry Price.

In the end, this was an easy enough resolution to make. That left only the question of how to put it into practice.

The London I was inhabiting – the London of the West End, smart streets, and respectable gentlemen – was still alien to me, for all that my new wealth was making me increasingly acquainted with it. But there was another London I knew from my days as a sailor. That was the London where I had first met James Brooke – the London of the docks. I may have put my fighting days behind me, but I would have no difficulty in finding men who would stand at my back if I took a few drinks in my old haunts.

My first move must be to purchase some more appropriate clothes. Were I to arrive at a dockside tavern dressed as I was, I would be more likely to fall victim to the predations of some well-muscled seamen than to have the opportunity to recruit such men to my cause.

It was too late to buy anything that day, but early the next morning I was on my way to the East of the town. Near the Pool of London, between the chandleries and the warehouses, the taverns and the stores selling dry biscuits and salt pork, there were a few shops where you could buy 'slops', as the garments worn by sailors were known. The shirt and waistcoat I purchased were not so different in style from those that I had bought in Plymouth, but they were made of duck-cloth – more like canvas than the fine linen of my other clothes. My clothes would be amongst the best on display in the tavern where I proposed to recruit my helpers, but at least they would be sailor's garb and not a gentleman's. I bought bell-bottomed trousers, easier to be rolled up when running barefoot about the deck and up and down the rigging, and a jacket in fashionable blue – fashionable, that is, amongst seamen. I wondered whether to retain my top hat, for top hats have become the uniform of the working man and even common sailors have abandoned the bandana of my youth. In the end, though, I decided on a new hat too. My Plymouth-bought hat was silk and a plain felt finish seemed more sensible alongside the rest of my clothing.

The shopman made a parcel of my purchases, neatly folded and tied around with string. If he was curious as to why somebody so apparently prosperous was buying such items, he thought it better not to ask. In any case, while a gentleman's tailor would expect to be given an address for delivery and details as to how the account should be rendered, in the slop shop affairs were conducted strictly on the basis of payment in cash and the purchaser to collect the goods.

Feeling somewhat conspicuous with my substantial parcel under my arm, I set out to return immediately to my hotel. Foolishly, perhaps, I had not asked the cab to wait while I made my purchases. As I emerged into the narrow lane where the shop was situated, I looked in vain for any sign of a vehicle for hire. Recalling the area from my youth, though, I knew that my best hope was to head towards the docks themselves, where cabmen will wait in the hope of finding fares from officers or gentlemen with business in the docks or even, perhaps, from sailors rich on their discharge pay.

I doubt I had ever been in this exact spot before and the alleys and lanes formed a tangled maze, but I set off unhesitatingly towards the river. Any sailor, however long since he forsook service before the mast, can follow his nose to the sea – or, in this case, towards such of the docks as had not yet been sealed away behind the high new walls that the authorities happily believed would stop the depredations of the criminal fraternity.

Arriving at the river front, I looked out across a forest of masts. I must admit that, for a moment, I felt a kind of nostalgia for the days when I would have signed on with one of those vessels and set sail to who knew where. Then I remembered the voyages to Newcastle, the ferocity of a North Sea gale, the drunken captains and the thuggish mates, and the vermin in the ships' biscuits. The life of a sailor was hard, dangerous and, all too often, short. I had put those days behind me many years ago and I would not go to sea again, even as a passenger.

The wharves were busy with people coming and going and I soon found a cab to carry me to Paddington. I was back in my hotel before mid-morning with several hours to spend as I wished. I could not advance my scheme to recruit a couple of handy fellows until the evening, for such as I was seeking would not be ashore and idle in the afternoon. I needed men who were reliable and, as with any other sort of business, it is best to hire people who are generally in gainful employment, rather than rely on those who have been rejected by other masters.

I decided that I would set out again around six. That was, I accept, somewhat early for the kind of business I intended, but I did not wish to stay too late near the Pool.

Even in the broad light of the morning, I had been accosted by half-a-dozen whores on my short walk from shop to dock and I had observed their pimps lurking in the alleys. The clothes I had bought were too smart and new not to draw attention. I might not be dressed as a gentleman, but, if I appeared a sailor, it was still a sailor with money – and a pimp may separate a moneyed sailor from his purse with a knife, if the arts of his whores cannot achieve the same end more subtly.

I passed the time with a stroll in Hyde Park. The great Crystal Palace was gone, of course, but I imagined the place swarming with visitors come to see the wonders of our Empire. Today, it was quieter, though there were couples taking the air together. It seemed a popular place for servants on a half-holiday to meet with their beaus. It was certainly very respectable, with the Keepers making a regular patrol. Altogether, I had such a pleasant stroll that I almost forgot my errand.

It felt strange changing into the clothes that I had bought that morning. Pulling on the heavy canvas of the shirt took me back to the time when such fabric had been my daily wear. Now it scratched against my skin. The bell-bottoms seemed ridiculous and the blue of the jacket garish.

Once dressed I positively scurried out of the hotel, conscious of the astonished glances of the staff as I passed. Fortunately, London's cabmen are undiscriminating in their choice of fare and I engaged a cab with no difficulty. I directed it to take me towards the Pool, where I asked to be dropped a hundred yards or so from a likely tavern that I had noticed that morning.

The unimaginatively named Sailor's Arms reminded

me of the place where I had first met James Brooke. It was, as dockside taverns go, a respectable house. The sawdust that was spread across the floor had clearly been replaced that day. The serving women, if revealing rather more décolletage than was strictly proper, were not openly offering their favours to the clientele and there were no unaccompanied women looking for business on the premises.

The customers reflected the atmosphere of the house. Their clothes showed them to be either sailors or stevedores. They were drinking quietly this early in the evening and none was drunk. I thought that there would probably be people there who could serve my purpose.

I had hardly sat down when one of the women was at my elbow asking what I would have and once I had told her, a pint of ale was soon on the table in front of me. I sipped it slowly. Nothing was to be gained by hurrying. The commission I had in mind, while not illegal, was not entirely proper either. It was best to settle in and wait to be approached, rather than to impose myself on the company.

Men who work on the sea are a gregarious bunch. It was not long before a new arrival chose to sit at my table and by the time I had finished my pint I had three new friends who were all cheerfully telling me about which ships they were signed on with and when they next expected to leave port.

I could tell they were curious about me. My hands weren't stained with the tar of the rigging and my appearance belied my dress. I was not fresh off a ship, and they knew it.

I did not lie to them, though I did not feel it necessary to tell them the whole truth. I explained that I had, indeed, worked as a sailor, but that I had come into money (I gave no idea of how much) and that I had given up the sea, at least for now. I had, though, the need of some assistance and was looking for somebody who might be willing to help a fellow seaman. Did anybody have shore leave the next day and a desire to earn a sovereign or two?

As I had already ascertained that none were due to sail for three days, I was confident that at least one would be more than willing to make a profit from their shore leave. In the event, two remarked that a sovereign was always useful and asked me how they could earn it.

So it was that the next day found me back at Seven Dials with two large men at my back.

Even with this escort, I must admit that I was nervous as I entered that noisome slum. I had decided to start at Broad Street, where I had had my first sight of the place. It was, as so often had been the case of late, a warm day and I could have sworn that the miasma that hung about the sewage-clogged drains was visible in the air. Walking down Great St Andrews Street into the heart of the rookery, it was as if we inhaled the evil genius of Seven Dials with every breath we took.

In broad daylight and with my two protectors in close attendance, no one made any step to interfere with us as we walked down the street. From Broad Street the road we were now walking down seemed a straightforward passage of some few hundred yards. Once inside the rookery, though, I found the shabby – nay, decrepit – frontage of dirty, straggling houses, interrupted every now and then by an unexpected court. These yards, leading off from what I suppose I should call the main thoroughfare, seemed, if possible, even more miserable than Great St Andrews Street itself. In one, the ground was covered with pieces of brickwork that seemed to have fallen from the surrounding buildings, while another had a pool of sewage marking its centre like an ornamental pond. As we passed, a half-naked urchin was squatting down and adding to it.

In one yard a goat wandered among the rubbish, poking here and there in search of food. It must have found something edible there, for it looked remarkably healthy –

more than could be said of most of the people that I saw peering from alleys or glancing quickly through the empty panes of windows.

As we moved down the road we passed bakers' shops, the smell of fresh bread incongruous in that fetid atmosphere. A druggist's was invitingly adorned with beautiful green and purple jars, but there was no sign of any customers. I found myself wondering what sort of person might patronise such an establishment, when I saw a man splendidly dressed in frock coat and with a fine beaver hat upon his head. On his arm was a girl in a fashionable blue dress, but the marks of the pox were already visible on her features. As I watched, I saw her point at a cake in the baker's window and her companion went straightway in and coins were drawn from a bulging purse. It occurred to me that there was money in Seven Dials, but it seemed likely that it was not honestly come by and it did not stay long in the pockets of those who obtained it.

We arrived safely at a little plinth that marked the centre of the neighbourhood. Here there had once stood a pillar with the seven sundials that gave Seven Dials its name, but the pillar was long gone. Only a few stones, too low even for a mounting block, remained in the middle of this square. Not that the area was square. It marked the spot where seven streets met. In whatever direction you faced, sharply angled buildings stabbed towards you. The effect was disorienting, for each street looked the same. Furthermore at this confluence, all the buildings that the traveller found himself looking at were public houses. Only dirty street signs, high on the walls of the narrow roads, provided any clue as to the direction that you should follow.

Three young men were loitering at one of these corners, attired as mechanics or tradesmen, though their dress was shabby in the extreme. They looked at us with the air of

37

men on the outlook for booty and I cast about for the safest path to take us rapidly away from that spot, for it seemed to me that it would be easy for a crowd to gather here within minutes. My two bruisers, however menacing an air they might attempt, could only offer me so much protection. I was about to strike off at random – for it seemed more important to exude an impression of confidence than to worry unduly as to the road – when I made out the name of Queen Street on a dirty plate attached precariously to the side of one of the public houses. I struck out straightaway into that thoroughfare, my two guardian angels following close behind.

I had not been given a house number at which to enquire for Harry Price and, now that I was in Queen Street, the reason for the omission became clear. None of the houses bore any indication of their number. This was hardly surprising: door knockers, bell pulls, handles – all seem to have been stripped away. In several of the houses the doors themselves were gone. There was no chance that anything so esoteric as a brass number would have survived the depredations of those who were clearly stripping the properties for scrap.

A child stepped down from the pavement and, standing a moment before me in the roadway, rolled his eyes at me and stuck out his tongue before darting back into one of the houses, slamming the door behind him. A few seconds later, I saw him reappear from a doorway three or four houses further up the street. It appeared that, although the houses had been built as separate residences, they were now connected inside to form a single warren.

Another child was standing behind us. I had not seen him arrive in the street: it was as if he had materialised out of the fetid air. More of the wretched creatures appeared, shoeless and ragged. Some wore jackets, or, despite the heat, old tattered coats, much too large for them. Others displayed dirty shirts, their ragged trousers hanging by one brace. There were girls, too: some in old, dirty pinafores and others in petticoats. All of them were filthy, their hair – when not cropped to their scalps – plastered in wild disorder like so many mops or hanging down in dishevelled locks. I should have been moved to pity, but as the children surrounded my little party I had to admit that my primary emotion was fear. My two seamen obviously shared my concerns for they moved closer to me.

We edged further down the street as the children moved nearer, until, surrounded, we came to a halt.

One of the ragamuffins, a little older than the others – I guessed him to be ten or twelve years of age – seemed to be their spokesman and placed himself firmly in my path.

'Wot you doin' 'ere? You don't belong 'ere.'

There was an unmistakable belligerence in his tone and I felt, rather than saw, my two companions reaching for the billy clubs I knew they had concealed in their jackets. A street brawl, though, would hardly serve my purpose, so I gestured for them to remain calm, while I explained to my young interlocutor that we had come in search of Harry Price.

'Wot do you want with 'Arry?'

I allowed myself an inward sigh of relief that the name was familiar to him and that, if his tone still remained antagonistic, at least there was no immediate threat of violence. I replied that he had been a childhood friend – not exactly the truth, but close enough for these purposes.

The lad looked unconvinced by my account, but, remaining planted firmly in my way, he nodded to one of the other children. 'Go an' get 'Arry. Tell him there's a bloke here as sez,' (there was a definite scepticism in that last word), 'sez as 'e knows 'im.'

I stood for what seemed an age, waiting in the roadway, surrounded by twenty or thirty children, most under the age of ten. It was, as I have mentioned, a hot day, and the wholesome smell of baking bread seemed already a distant memory. Where I stood, with street urchins on all sides, the unwashed bodies of the young delinquents added to the ripeness of the street smells, making an already unpleasant situation even more distasteful.

I was, yet again, thinking that I had been a fool to start on this errand and that I should take myself back to Bickleigh at the earliest opportunity, when I saw a man emerge from one of the doors a little way down the street.

'You clear off, lads, and leave this to me.' The unmistakeable Devonian burr sounded strange in that London slum, but there was a reassurance in the tone. Harry Price, whoever he was, did not sound like a villain.

The ring of boys around us moved back a few paces, but they were not about to abandon their morning's entertainment.

A break appeared in the circle and Harry stepped towards me. He was a stocky fellow. I judged him to be in his early thirties, with the air of a man used to working with his hands. He seemed somehow out of place wearing the dark suit and hat that seemed obligatory for all classes of men in London, even here amongst the very poorest. I felt he should have been wearing a labourer's smock and standing bare-headed in an open field, not trammelled in a London slum.

'Do I know thee?'

'No, but you know a friend of mine, Michael Radford.'

'Aye.' He strung the syllable out, infusing the word with uncertainty and suspicion.

'My name is John Williamson. I knew him as a child in Bickleigh. I left almost thirty years ago, but now I'm back. They said in Bickleigh that he had followed you to London and I promised Mrs Slattery that I would bring her news of him.'

It was a tangled sort of explanation, but I saw his face twitch in recognition of Mrs Slattery's name. It was that, I think, that persuaded him to beckon me to follow him. The three of us trailed him down the street and entered one of the houses on the right-hand side. It seemed, so far as I could judge, a trifle less dilapidated than some of its neighbours. There was a door that was still attached to the frame and the windows to the street, protected by iron bars, were unbroken. Inside, though, the narrow hallway was dark and smelled of damp, but once the door was closed some of the stench of sewage was shut out.

I judged there must be some sort of basement, for I heard movement below us, but Price hurried me along the hall towards the stairs that ran steeply upwards. 'Be careful,' he warned. 'Some of the treads are missing.' I took him at his word and exercised caution in where I placed my feet. Most of the steps were safe enough, but some were, as he had warned, completely missing. The gaps did not look like the effects of wear or casual damage, but rather as if they had been deliberately removed. As we turned a corner on the stair, Price looked back and saw the puzzlement on my face. 'We take some out so that a Peeler running up will fall. We know which steps to take, so we can race up without any inconvenience. It can be useful if there's a raid.' I must still have looked confused for he grinned and added, 'Anyway, we burn them for fuel in the winter.'

He opened the door to a room on the first floor. 'First floor back,' he said. 'Practically the best room in the house.'

It seemed strange in that wretched building, but he opened the door as proudly as any tenant introducing guests to a rented room anywhere. I stepped forward and entered.

I paused for a moment, barely crediting what I was seeing. Outside was filth and decrepitude but inside was a picture of respectable domesticity. It was clear that Price lived in just the one room, for a neatly made-up bed was set against one wall. Most of the rest of the space was taken up by a deal table, which I judged to be a rare and precious thing in a house where it seemed the very stair treads had been taken up for fuel. It was scrubbed clean and in the middle, in a little chipped pot, was a bunch of flowers. They were drooping, it is true, and I judged them to be the last of some flower-child's stock, too sad to be sold the next day, but they brought a cheerful touch of colour to the place. There was no glass in the windows, but in the summer warmth that was scarcely a concern and some scraps of cloth had been nailed to the frame to give the appearance of curtains.

On the wall opposite the door was a grate, the metal surround of which had been painted a gleaming white. A mirror, still bright for all that there was some speckling on it, stood proudly above the fireplace in a rosewood frame.

Two plain wooden chairs were tucked neatly under the table and Price gestured to one. My escort had chosen to remain outside, where they could watch the approach to the door, so Price took the other seat.

'I should offer you tea,' he said, 'but we have a common kitchen here and you'll pardon me not leaving you while I go and make a new pot.'

'No matter.' I looked about and smiled my approval. 'You seem quite set up here.'

'Yes. I could have done a lot worse.' There was a pause that threatened to become uncomfortable and then we both opened our mouths to speak together. I sat back, gesturing that he should talk first.

'You were wanting news of Michael.'

'Yes. Mrs Slattery is concerned not to have heard from him. She asked me to enquire and find out if he is well. I believe he came here to see you.'

As I spoke, a smile made its way across Harry Price's face. He was a good-enough looking fellow, but that smile transformed him and I think it was then that I began to have the first inkling of what had occurred.

'Yes. He came. Said he had heard as I was in trouble and he came to look out for me.'

My first thought was simply to ask whether Price could tell me where Michael had gone, but that smile made me uneasy, so I simply asked what had happened.

'Well …' He looked around the room as if seeing it as a stranger would and then he shrugged. 'You have to know that I did not always live like this.'

'I know. You were in Devon.'

His glance silenced me. I realised I had been foolish to interrupt and I gestured him to continue.

'Yes, I was in Devon. And I came here certain that a man with ambition could better himself in London.' He stopped, silent for a moment, a rueful half-smile on his face. 'Well, I soon learned better. In Bickleigh, I was known as a good worker. Here no one knew me. I had no trade and, without that, masters laughed and sent me away. I thought that there would always be a place for a strong pair of hands, but they said I was too old. Too old! I am thirty-three years of age and here in London they call that "old".'

I said nothing. Now that I thought it, most of the people that I saw scurrying busily about the streets were, I suppose, what I would call young, but at my time of life so many people seem young. Harry and I sat for a moment, silently contemplating the march of years, uncomfortably reminded of our mortality.

'It became all too clear that I had no chance of honest work, but I could not bear to return to Bickleigh and admit the foolishness of my attempt to build a new life here. And what does Bickleigh offer? To find a girl who will wed me and then to work in the fields to keep a family until I am truly old and can work no longer?'

It was, I thought, the life that most of my childhood companions would have had, and accounted themselves as happy as most men had a right to be. But there was something about the curl of his lip when he spoke of a wife that, again, made me wonder if Harry Price and I had more in common than he realised.

He took up his tale, explaining how, once his money had run out ('And that was sooner than I had thought, for London is a dreadful expensive place to live'), he had been unable to afford even the meanest of lodging houses and had gravitated by a sort of osmosis to the rookery of Seven Dials. 'For you see, there is no rent to pay on these rooms.'

'So you just moved in and set up your home here?'

'Well, no. It was not quite that simple.' He reached towards the little pot of flowers and drew it to him, fiddling with it with long fingers that seemed somehow feminine and out of keeping with the rest of his anatomy. 'I found a corner in a cellar.'

I thought of the sewage in the street outside. I could scarcely imagine what conditions in the cellar must have been like.

'I had a few pennies left for food, but the first night, those were stolen from me. That's when I realised that I had to go back to Devon.'

He told me that part of the story that I already knew: how he had tried to board the train without a ticket, been taken up by the police, and spent a few days in their cells.

'After that, what could I do? I came back here. There was nowhere else to go.'

His time in the cells, it seemed, served as something of a character reference for the denizens of Seven Dials. He was allowed to take up his place in the cellar once again and even approached with offers of, if not employment exactly, then opportunities to make money.

'It started with begging,' he explained. 'I had tried my luck before.'

He fiddled with the pot again. 'It was shaming, but I was hungry, sir. It was that or starve. But every time I put my hat upon the ground, I would be moved on.'

'By the police?'

'No, sir, by the other beggars.'

There were, it seemed, laws which governed the lives of such as lived in Seven Dials – laws that the honest men and women of London could never be aware of, but which were imposed by the poor upon each other. Price had fallen foul of the rules that govern begging. The city, it seemed, was divided into pitches, and each pitch was assigned to a single beggar. In exchange for a few pennies, paid to an enforcer, the mendicant would be left to ply his trade without competition. Should the money not be forthcoming, though, his pitch would be assigned to another.

'I said I had as much right to beg there as he did and suddenly there were three or four of them, and one man who looked like no beggar I had ever seen and who stood by and watched as the others beat me until I fled. I had salvaged a few pennies in my flight and it was those that were stolen from me that night.'

After his appearing at the police court, though, it seemed that he was considered fit to join the fraternity of London beggars. He had no sooner left the cellar after his first night back in the place once the police had released him, than the man who had watched him beaten accosted him in Queen Street.

'I was terrified, as you can well imagine, and I turned to flee, but he took me by the shoulder and told me there should be no hard feelings, but that he would try me on a pitch near Holborn and see how I got on. As I was, he said, on probation, I was to give him half of my takings for the day, but he would put me under his protection and I would not be robbed again.'

The bully had at least been true to his word and so Price had joined the army of organised beggars. It seemed, though, that he was not successful as a beggar. He was a fit and healthy man in his thirties and, though the reality of his situation was that he could not find gainful employment, he would not have seemed a deserving case to the gentlemen who passed him sitting by the road in Holborn. He seemed, therefore, doomed to remain forever in a corner of that miserable cellar begging just enough to keep body and soul together until the filth and squalor destroyed his health.

It was at this point that Michael found him.

'I was ashamed,' he said – and, if I had any doubt as to the sincerity of his emotion, the tears in his eyes would have convinced me. 'Michael wanted me to return with him to Bickleigh, but I knew that word of my disgrace had got back to Devon and I could not bear to face the people who once knew me.'

At this point, Price stopped his story and, holding the cracked pot in his hands, gazed at the little posy without speaking. I waited, reluctant to interrupt his tale again, but he remained silent. Eventually, I felt forced to say something.

'So what happened to Michael?'

His face twisted. I could not read his thoughts, but he was clearly in the grip of some intense emotion. At last, he said, 'I cannot tell you.'

'He is lost!' I was surprised by the intensity of my own feelings. Until that moment, I had convinced myself that my expedition to find Michael Radford was incidental to my visit to London, undertaken simply to gratify Mrs Slattery. Now, though, I realised how much I wanted to see my childhood friend. To have come so close, and then lost him!

I felt Price's eyes on me and I sought to regain my composure. 'Mrs Slattery will be disappointed.'

Price had pushed the pot back to the centre of the table and now sat carefully upright, his hands flat on the scrubbed deal. 'He is not lost.'

'Then tell me where I can find him.'

Again, Price's face took on that troubled look. He frowned, yet I could see a hint of a smile about his lips. 'Perhaps it is better if I tell him where he can find you.'

'I'm at the Royal Hotel at Paddington.'

'No, not your hotel. Somewhere …' He paused in thought. Then: 'Do you know Hyde Park?'

'I was there only yesterday, where the Crystal Palace used to stand.'

'Ah, that will do,' he said, and the Devonshire burr was suddenly more obvious as he relaxed. 'Why don't you wait there at about midday tomorrow and Michael will find you?'

As he spoke, he was already rising to his feet. He was courteous, but it was clear that he did not want to talk with me any further, so, thanking him, I left and made my way carefully down the staircase. My escort fell in behind me and we walked those noxious streets until Seven Dials was behind us and, with relief, we found ourselves on Oxford Street and back in the world of civilised London.

CHAPTER FOUR

The spell of warm, dry weather showed no signs of coming to an end, and the next morning found me strolling amongst the crowds enjoying the air in the park.

I was aware of a certain ridiculous melodrama to the situation, but I found it amusing rather than alarming. Harry Price obviously lived cheek by jowl with a criminal underworld where I imagined anything as straightforward as calling upon a man at his hotel was almost superstitiously avoided. Besides, it was clear, just looking around the park, that meeting in public places was normal amongst the working classes. There is an enormous servant class in London who cannot entertain in their masters' and mistresses' homes and those fortunate enough to have homes of their own will likely have limited opportunities to receive their friends in private. The park, in consequence, was dotted with young couples or older men who would raise their hats politely upon meeting and then stroll alongside each other while discussing whatever business had brought them together.

I made sure to arrive early at the Crystal Palace site and settle myself on one of the benches provided for the convenience of the public. Behind me the traffic rattled up and down the Kensington Road, but I looked out over green lawns with the tree-lined avenues of Kensington Gardens in the distance. All was quiet and ordered. The scene was that of a city at ease with itself, enjoying the prosperity that came with being the beating heart of an Empire that spanned the globe. It was a world away from Seven Dials, though less than three miles separated me from that hell on earth.

I drew the watch from my fob pocket, for the open vista offered neither clock nor sundial. It wanted fifteen minutes until noon, so I settled myself to wait, but barely five minutes had passed when a figure approaching along the path from my right caught my eye. It was Michael Radford.

He was, of course, a middle-aged man by now, as was I, but I recognised him straight away. His hair was speckled with grey and his face had lines upon it that had never been there when I knew him in Bickleigh, but his eyes were the same dark blue and I remembered that smile. I wondered, then, if I remembered it rather too well, but, as he walked towards me, his hand extended in greeting, I put that thought from me.

'John Williamson, as I live and breathe. I haven't seen you these thirty years.'

'Twenty-eight years, Michael.'

He laughed. 'You always were one to take care in your reckoning.' He took a step back and looked me over from head to toe, taking in the clothes I was wearing, for I was not dressed in canvas today.

'Well, your reckoning must have been sound indeed, to have done as well as you have. You're dressed like a gentleman, John.'

'I suppose I am a gentleman, Michael.' And then, without thinking, I blurted out, 'I'm thinking of buying The Grange.'

As soon as I had said it, I wished I had not. Michael was respectably enough dressed, with suit, waistcoat and hat. But his shoes were scuffed and his collar was frayed.

'So now you're rich, you've come to bring Mrs Slattery's charity to the poor, have you, John?'

'Good God, man, don't be so stupid.' I stepped forward to embrace him, but he moved away.

'I got my money in the Far East. And now I'm back in

England and you are the first face that I've known or that has known me. Don't shun me, Michael, because I can buy a good suit.'

He hesitated. 'A nabob, then?' he said.

'After a fashion. I served in Borneo with James Brooke and after that I was in India. I was at Cawnpore during the Mutiny.'

It was a calculated play for his sympathy and I despised myself for it, but I could not bear him to be angry and leave me.

'You were at Cawnpore? I thought all but four of them died.'

'Some of us were not in the town when the uprising started.' I fudged the truth: nothing was to be gained by telling that story now. 'They gave me a pension and sent me home.'

He was staring at me now, as if I were some marvel or a strange new creature in the zoo.

'It was a very generous pension,' I said. 'That and the money from Borneo is why I might be accounted a gentleman.' I gestured at my fine new clothes and shrugged. 'I bought them less than a week ago.'

The admission that my clothes were practically brand new finally drew a smile to Michael's lips.

'Well, perhaps I had better not judge you too harshly, then,' he said, and sat himself down beside me. 'Tell me what you've been doing.'

'What? Twenty-eight years and a journey halfway around the world? That will take a while, Michael, and I think will have to wait for another day. But what of yourself? I know what you were doing until a few months ago. What's happened to you since you arrived in London?'

'Oh, you know, mustn't grumble.'

He couldn't have looked shiftier if he'd tried. I was damned if I was going to help him out. I just sat there and waited.

After a while he added: 'You know I found Harry Price.'

'Yes.' I still wasn't going to help.

'Well, he needed a hand.'

'It seems so.'

Michael Radford gave me a sharp look at my tone. 'I had to help him. I couldn't just leave him there.'

'But what happened, Michael? Harry said he couldn't tell me. You seem to have done a great deal for him, so why the mystery? What are you doing here in London? How do you earn your bread? Where do you live?'

Michael shook his head, as if he could hardly believe his ears. 'You really don't know, do you?'

'No, I don't. Are you in trouble?'

He turned to look towards me. He had looked at me before, of course, as anyone would look at a friend they had not seen for so many years. But now he stared into my face, as if trying to search out my soul.

'You could say that,' he said.

'Then let me get you back to Bickleigh. The money you so despise me for may as well be put to some good use and I know Mrs Slattery will be glad to see you home and help you get back on your feet there.'

'I'm not going back to Bickleigh. Harry won't go and I won't leave without him.'

'Harry seems to be doing well, now. I'm sure he can manage on his own.'

Michael barked out a noise, somewhere between a laugh and a howl. A gentleman sitting on the bench to our right turned and looked at us.

'I can't talk like this,' Michael said. 'Let's take a stroll through the gardens and we can talk as we walk.'

We set off towards the wooded paths of Kensington Gardens and, as we walked, Michael gradually told me his story.

His first idea was to get himself a job and, once he was established, to use some of his money to find decent accommodation for his friend. All too soon, he realised that what had been true of Harry was even truer of him. He was in his forties and, although he was still a big, barrel-chested man barely past his prime, no one in London was interested in offering him employment. Like Harry, he saw his money running out, but unlike Harry, his visits to Queen Street meant that he had friends in Seven Dials.

'Charlie – he's the fellow who owns the house – he said he could probably put a bit of work my way.'

'What sort of work? Harry told me that most of the men there are reduced to begging.'

Michael gave a humourless grin. 'Aye, for most of them that's true. But I look too strong to beg. No, Charlie thought he could use me as one of his bullies.'

It took a moment for the implications of this to sink in. Was this "Charlie" the man who had led the attack on Harry Price? I had promised myself I would not pass judgement on Michael if he admitted to being drawn into the criminal activities that made up the economic life of Seven Dials. Even so, I was shocked at the idea that he might have become one of those who preyed upon the most miserable of their fellow men.

He must have seen the expression on my face, for he hastened to reassure me. 'Don't worry – I didn't do it.'

Michael had explained that after his friend had been beaten, he was uncomfortable with getting involved with that sort of work. 'Charlie thought I was being what he called "sentimental", but he understood my feelings. He said he'd look out for something else.'

'Something else' had eventually turned up. Charlie, it appeared, had a friend who was a coiner.

'The thing about coining,' Michael explained, 'is that you don't just have to make the coins, you have to pass them off afterwards.'

The counterfeiter would pass coins out through men such as Charlie, who would buy them at a substantial discount.

'Charlie's mate was making shillings and he sold each coin for a penny. Then Charlie would pass them to people he knew in Seven Dials who would buy them off him for tuppence on the shilling. Those were the people who would pass the tin off as real, generally. You have to give them the shillings cheap, because there's a lot of risk of being caught passing money. Shopkeepers are wise to the likes of us and check the coin careful.'

Michael, being new to Seven Dials, still looked hale and healthy. The people I had seen in that neighbourhood were generally pathetic specimens, half-starved and worn down by disease and rough living. 'Charlie put a decent coat on me and I went out to spend his money. I was not known to the traders, so they were less wary of me. I would go out and buy food and necessaries and Charlie would sell them to the fellows in his houses and that meant, even selling cheap, he could make nine or ten pence on every shilling.'

'Once or twice,' he admitted, he had been challenged. 'It didn't signify,' he said. 'I got away.' I looked at him, his hands clenched unconsciously in remembrance of his 'getting away'. He was still a big man.

'Charlie said he was really pleased with my work. He said that it would make sense if we did all the work, from making the coins through to passing them off.'

Coining was a common enough crime, and easy to do. 'You can make the moulds yourself, but Charlie said it made more sense to take some ready made for us.' Michael paused at this point in his account and I felt he was uncertain how much to tell me, but, after a moment, he plunged on. 'Charlie sent me with a few mates to explain the situation to the geezer who had been selling us the tin. He saw the sense of it, and even made us a gift of some of the moulds.'

Again came that grin. It was all too easy to imagine what had taken place.

Charlie had decided to set up the coining operation in the cellars. Of course, that meant the men who had been sleeping there – and women too, for there was an equality of the sexes when it came to misery and degradation – would have to find alternative accommodation. Part of Michael's reward for his contribution towards Charlie's burgeoning empire was that Harry would be allocated the back bedroom where he now lived. It was, as Michael put it, 'A big step up in the world for Harry.'

Harry's advancement owed everything to Michael's value to Charlie. As he talked, it became obvious that Charlie was relying on him to run the coining operation on his behalf.

Though I had resolved not to condemn Michael for any criminal acts he may have been involved in, I became increasingly worried as he began to detail the work that he had been doing for Charlie. He had an obvious excuse for his behaviour, for it was clear that Harry's new life depended on Michael's work. While Charlie considered Michael a valuable member of his coining gang, Harry could live in his back bedroom in peace. If Michael were to cross his 'employer', though, it was clear his friend would suffer. As far as I was concerned, though, I wanted no part of it and I was uncomfortable with the casual way in which, it seemed to me, Michael was drawing me into his world. I had no wish to know the details of the coiner's art.

'Enough of this!' I said. 'Is this to be your life henceforth? Would you not welcome the chance to return to Bickleigh and an honest life among your friends?'

I had, perhaps, spoken more harshly than I had intended and my companion responded in kind.

'Would you have me leave the life I have made in

London to return to Devon and work in the fields until I am old and my body is broken? And what friends do I have there to compare with the friend ...' he hesitated and then spoke on, 'the friends I have here?'

'You have friends aplenty. Mrs Slattery, for one, is concerned for your welfare.'

By now, Michael was as angry as when he had first taken me for a rich gentleman. Clearly he believed that Mrs Slattery was patronising him and that I was, in my turn, condescending in telling him of her concern. He responded to my comment with harsh and unkind words and I thought he would turn from me and leave. I put my hand on his arm, but he shook it off.

'Don't let us part angry, Michael,' I said.

He grunted something in reply; I couldn't make out what. Still, he did not leave, so I tried again.

'Let me know where I can find you, and we can meet again, when we are both calmer. Perhaps I could buy you some lunch.'

It was the wrong thing to say, again. He told me that he had no need of my charity and could buy his own lunch. Then, before I could seek to detain him again, he strode away. After a few paces, though, as if regretting his impetuosity he turned and spoke. 'If you truly want to find me again, send word by Harry Price. But do not expect me to return with you to Bickleigh, for I am determined against it.' Then, once more striding out towards Kensington Road, he was gone.

I could have followed, but to what purpose? Everything I said had been wrong and, it seemed, the more I spoke, the more I must drive a wedge between us. With a heavy heart, I made my way back North across the park and found an eating house on Bayswater Road where I sat alone to a cheerless lunch.

My mission on Mrs Slattery's behalf had ended in failure. My childhood friend was, it seemed, a friend no longer. I would spend a few days in the capital, stroll down Piccadilly, visit the Tower and St Paul's Cathedral and maybe Madame Tussaud's waxworks. I thought I might even see if I could obtain entrance to the Strangers' Gallery at the House of Commons. I knew little of England's political life after so long away, but, even since I had landed in Plymouth, there had been a change of government, and I thought I should at least feign interest in Palmerston's machinations.

All this should fill my time entertainingly enough for a week or so. I would send word to Michael Radford before I returned to Devon and suggest we share a pint or two for old times' sake, but I would not be so stupid as to make any further suggestion that he accompany me.

I resolved to start my round of sightseeing with a visit to the Zoological Gardens that very afternoon and so I hailed a cab (easily enough, for they were plentiful on Kensington Road) and took myself to Regent's Park and spent a few hours admiring the elephants and enjoying the chatter of the monkeys.

It was not until eight in the evening that I arrived back at my hotel, intending to dine there and then retire to bed. I collected my key at the desk and made my way slowly, for it had been a long afternoon at the zoo, up the grand staircase towards my room.

I was not aware of being followed upstairs, but as I unlocked my door I felt a hand on my shoulder. I turned to protest, but, before I could do so, the man who had accosted me spoke with a voice of quiet authority.

'I am officer of the law, sir. I would appreciate a few minutes of your time.'

By now he had been joined by another gentleman, both smartly dressed and apparently inoffensive, but somehow menacing in their demeanour. Although he had spoken as if making a request, I did not really feel that I was being offered a choice. I opened the door and the three of us trooped in.

I had a comfortable room, but there were only two chairs. I gestured that my uninvited guests should take these, while I made to sit on the bed.

'That's all right, sir. You have a chair. My colleague and I are happy to stand.'

I sat, somewhat reluctantly. What had been presented as a simple courtesy left me sitting while the two strangers stood over me. It was not a comfortable position and I responded with a show of bluster.

'You say you are officers of the law, yet you wear no uniforms. Do you have any evidence of your authority?'

The gentleman who had spoken to me seemed to be the more senior of the two, the other remaining silent and standing fractionally further off. Now he withdrew a wallet from the pocket of his jacket and, from the wallet, a piece of printed card, which he passed over to me. Beneath a crest showing the lion and the unicorn, it read, *The holder of this card is engaged in work of the highest importance. Please render them any assistance possible.*

The signature under these two lines was barely legible, but neatly printed below it was the name of Sir George Cornewall Lewis. And then, for those of us like myself who had no idea who Sir George might be, the designation Home Secretary.

I was tempted to laugh and throw it in his face, for surely the card was some sort of practical joke, but one look at his expression showed me that he was deadly serious. I looked at the card again.

'I may have been a long time out of the country, sir, but I am not such a fool as to believe this a policeman's warrant card.'

'I didn't say I was a policeman, Mr Williamson. I said I was an officer of the law.'

I was somewhat taken aback that he knew my name, although, given that he clearly knew where I was staying, that was hardly surprising. My face must have registered my perturbation, for I saw a glint of satisfaction in his eyes as he continued. 'I work for a department of the Home Office that is concerned with maintaining the security of the country.'

'What has that to do with me? I have barely returned to England after a long absence.'

'We know about that, sir. You were with Sir James Brooke in Borneo, and then served with the East India Company at Cawnpore.'

It was clear, by now, that he said these things just to rattle me. I knew I should have remained calm, but I found it impossible not to respond.

'How do you know all these things? What business are my affairs of you?'

He allowed himself a smile. 'As to how we know these things, sir, it is our business to know things about people. But the reason that it is our business is that you have been visiting Queen Street.'

'What of it?'

'Well, sir, it's not the sort of place a gentleman like yourself would usually be seen. Might I ask what you were doing there?'

'I was making enquiries about a friend from my childhood.'

He drew a notebook from his pocket and made play of consulting it, though I am sure he did not need to. 'Michael Radford?'

I nodded.

He took a step nearer so that I, sitting in the hard-backed chair, found myself tilting my head back to look up at him. 'And what does Mr Radford do for a living?'

I shook my head. My interrogator, for that is what he seemed to be, turned to his companion. 'Mr Williamson appears a man of few words. A nod here, a shake of the head there.' He turned back to me. 'What does Michael

59

Radford do for a living?'

My mouth felt suddenly dry and I struggled to get a few words out. 'I don't know.'

'So what did you talk about with Mr Radford this morning?'

Suddenly Harry's insistence that I meet Michael in the park made sense. Obviously, though, this precaution had proved inadequate. Had we been watched all the time? Had our conversation been listened to? I blessed Michael for his insistence on walking about the gardens as we talked. We couldn't have been overheard.

'We talked about our childhood and my life in Borneo and India.'

'And nothing about his life here?' He did not trouble to conceal his scepticism.

'Nothing.'

He paused long enough for me to hope that my flat denial of the truth might be enough to send him on his way. I even began to rise from my chair to ask them to leave, but a firm hand on my shoulder pressed me gently down again.

'If you really don't know what Mr Radford is up to in Queen Street – and I do doubt that – then I will tell you. Michael Radford is a member – quite a senior member – of a gang of coiners.'

I did my best to look shocked. 'If that is truly the case, then his behaviour is, of course, criminal. But surely it is the business of police to put an end to such activities? I do not see that it is a matter concerning the security of the nation.'

'You have been engaged in public administration. You must understand the importance of sound currency.'

Of course I understood it. James Brooke had tutored me in the basics of economic theory as he had taught me to read and write and make up his accounts. 'We may not be a great nation,' he had said to me, 'but Sarawak is a nation, nonetheless, and it behoves us to understand these matters as much as it does the great men in Parliament at Westminster.' So I understood what 'sound money' meant and why coining was a Royal Offence. But the production of a few shillings, or even a few sovereigns, was hardly likely to threaten the stability of the nation's currency, which is why the crime was usually punished by only a few months – or a year or two – of imprisonment. It was hardly a matter of national security and I said as much to my interlocutor.

He looked at me without replying, as if trying to judge what I did or did not know about the going-on in Queen Street. He must have been satisfied with what he saw, for he stepped away and, for the first time, sat down in the other chair before speaking.

'It seems, sir, that the French do not agree with you.' He paused, as if awaiting a response, and when he did not get one, he continued. 'Our agents have intercepted a French plot. Unable to attack this country directly, they are planning an assault on our currency. It is the French, sir, who are behind the coining den on Queen Street. And that, sir, makes it treason.'

I was, as you can imagine, astonished at this suggestion, yet the mysterious 'officer of the law' was quite definite. 'The level of organisation that these people demonstrate is far greater than we see from regular coiners,' he explained. 'They are producing very considerable quantities of forged coins, all of a uniformly high quality.' They had, he argued, clearly been trained. But was there any evidence that they were connected to the French? The idea that Napoleon III was going to lead his troops across the Channel was, to my mind, an obvious nonsense, for all the volunteer militia claimed to expect to face the French any day. Was it really any more likely that Napoleon was waging economic warfare?

Apparently, the Home Office believed it to be the case.

And their evidence? 'Well, we've identified one of the ringleaders. He's a fellow they know as Charlie, but I prefer Sir Charles Crawley. He speaks French.'

That, apparently, was the core of their case against him. That, and the notion that, as Sir Charles was a baronet, he could not be involved in the affair for anything as vulgar as profit. The whole thing, it seemed to me, was mere fantasy, but the Home Office was taking it seriously. And, to my horror, they were insisting on involving me.

'We want Sir Charles before the courts on a treason charge, and we want the French ambassador to have to explain himself to Lord John Russell. We're keeping a close watch on these fellows, but they're damn' cunning. We've got no actual proof, you see – proof that would stand up in court. We need somebody working inside the gang – somebody Sir Charles would take into his confidence.'

That somebody, it seemed, was to be myself.

I expostulated. I protested. How could I possibly help them? Why would the coiners want to involve me in their undertaking?

'Sir Charles is the only one with any education, and that mainly Latin and Greek. And the French, of course.' He sniffed: a sniff that made quite clear what he thought of people who spoke French. 'He can't get help from our Gallic cousins on a day-to-day basis, for I'm sure he suspects we're watching him. He must be feeling very isolated by now. He'll like to have a man that he can talk to.'

'But why do you think he will talk to me?'

'You're a gentleman.' He looked me up and down, as if measuring every item of my wardrobe against some imaginary check-list, sniffed again, and added, 'Of a sort.'

I had had enough. I took advantage of his no longer standing over to me to get to my feet.

'I have had enough, sir. I have had enough of you and

your wretched plots and your insinuations and …'

I had forgotten about the other man, who had been standing silently near the door. Now he stepped forward and took me by the arm. I turned to shake him off, but, before I could do so, his colleague was speaking once again.

'Don't let's be hasty, Mr Williamson. I know what kind of man you are.'

There was no overt threat, but the air of menace in his voice left me in no doubt that it was a threat indeed. I fell silent and sat down again. You must remember that, at this time, sodomy was still punishable by death. I had only come to recognise the truth about my nature after I had left Britain and I had committed no criminal acts since my return, nor had I any intention of forming any more unnatural relationships. My conscience should have been clear, but to realise that this man knew, or seemed to know, the darkest secrets of my soul was inevitably disturbing.

He did not say anything to expand upon his remark, but he saw the effect of his words and appeared well satisfied with them. Leaning forward confidentially, he outlined his plan. 'You have friends already in Queen Street. Go to them and say that you would like to help them. Say that you exaggerated your wealth – that you have creditors and need to make some money quickly. Get involved with what they are doing. That is all that we ask.'

'All!' I was aghast. The idea that I should have anything to do with Seven Dials and its criminal fraternity appalled me. The gentleman – I use the term loosely – from the Home Office thought my response amusing.

'Yes, all. Think of it as an entertaining break from the mundanity of everyday life. It can't possibly be as exciting as your experiences in the Far East and there is not even any danger of a criminal charge – we'll take care of that. Why, Mr Williamson,' and now he reached out and slapped me on the shoulder, as if we were the oldest of friends, 'you could even stand to make some profit in the venture.'

CHAPTER FIVE

I was, as you can imagine, in some perturbation of mind once my uninvited visitors had left. I worried for some time as to the best course of action. Should I just leave London immediately and put the whole wretched situation behind me? That would mean never seeing Michael again ... Besides, why should I run from some anonymous functionary with his veiled threats? No, I would stay – but, in that case, it was surely wise to, at least, learn more of the situation in Queen Street. After all, I was curious on my own account and to return there committed me to nothing. What harm could it do? I would see Michael and might yet bring something good out of this whole unsavoury situation.

I resolved, then, to return to Seven Dials and make my peace with my old friend.

I went alone. If I were planning to represent myself as desirous of throwing in my lot with the coiners of Queen Street, then I could hardly turn up with bodyguards. Instead, I had to trust to the character that Harry Price had given me when he rescued me from the juvenile mob.

I must admit to some feeling of trepidation as, once again, I left the apparent safety of the West End streets and started down the dismal alleys of Seven Dials. My wariness of the denizens of that miserable ghetto was reciprocated. As I passed the men and women standing or sitting in twos and threes along the way, conversations stopped and I felt their eyes upon me. The ragged army of street urchins was mobilised, but they followed me at a respectable distance and no one interfered with my progress towards the house where I had left Mr Price.

I did not bother to knock on the door. It stood open and I doubted anyone within would have stirred from their rooms had I tapped at it. Instead I stepped inside as if I had every right to be there. The hallway was dark after the June sunlight outside, but I moved confidently towards the stairs. Before I reached them, though, a figure emerged from the gloom of one of the doorways that led onto the hall.

'Where the 'ell do you think you're going?'

I should, I realised, have reckoned on a guard, given the illicit activities that were carried on in these premises. Even if I had, though, I doubt I would have imagined such a man as this. He stood well over six feet tall and broad to match. His face was indistinct in the gloom, but, in any case, his features could hardly be seen for the great beard that grew in tangled profusion down over much of his chest.

I explained that my business was with Harry Price. The giant – for so he seemed to me – grunted, as if to acknowledge that he knew the name and that I might be speaking the truth, but he showed no signs of moving aside.

'I would speak with Mr Price,' I said. 'Will you let me pass?'

'I'll tell him you was 'ere. Wait in the Crown.'

It seemed I had no choice but to make my way to the public house at the end of the road.

The triangular shape of the building, occasioned by the peculiar arrangement of the streets, meant that the interior was well lit, despite the grime that covered the windows. Twenty or thirty people sat about the place or lay slumped over the tables, apparently sleeping. A couple of fellows were standing at the bar. They were being served not beer, but a clear liquid which, from the prevailing smell of the place, I recognised as gin.

As I watched, the men at the bar upended their glasses, downing the contents at a gulp, before making their way uncertainly to a space at one of the tables, where, regardless of the mess of crumbs and pooled liquor that stained it, they settled their heads upon the wood and promptly fell into a stuporous sleep.

Watching the scene, I paused, uncertain of whether or not to remain. The landlord, though, called across while I hesitated.

'What's your pleasure, sir?'

He spoke with a distinctly Irish lilt to his voice and I stepped hesitantly forward. 'A pint of beer?'

'We'll serve you beer willingly, sir.' He made his way to the beer pumps that lay at the farther end of the bar. 'We serve Wood Yard's here, sir, a fine beer and local. Do you know the brewery, sir?'

I confessed that I did not and he insisted on explaining exactly where it was. It stood, indeed, nearby and if the pervasive stench of the place was not so strong I would probably have smelt the distinctive aroma of beer being manufactured, but the brewery lay a little to the South and out of my way. 'It's a fine beer, sir, you must admit it,' he said, passing over a glass of some cloudy liquid which, once I sipped at it, I had to admit tasted a great deal better than it looked.

'You'll be wanting to sit with that,' he said.

I glanced around, but the two men who had been at the bar when I arrived seemed to have taken the last convenient seats. This did not worry the landlord, though, for he stepped from behind the bar and walked to one of the nearer tables where he proceeded to shake awake the man who was slumped there. 'It's time you were awake, Higgins. Will you have another glass?'

Higgins shook his head, gazing blearily around. He reached towards his trouser pocket and then, as if recollecting himself, shrugged. 'No money,' he mumbled.

'Then you'd best be on your way,' the landlord said, not unkindly and, taking Higgins firmly by the arm, he escorted him to the door.

I took the place he had vacated and concentrated on my beer, trying to ignore the stentorian snoring of the men on either side of me. I sipped slowly, anxious that I should not have finished before Harry had the chance to join me.

I need not have worried. Barely ten minutes after I had started my pint, Harry Price appeared at the door.

I beckoned him over, calling for the barman to provide another drink.

The barman poured Harry's beer and brought it to our table, nudging one of my neighbours awake and evicting him, as he had the unfortunate Higgins.

I raised my by now half-empty glass to Harry. 'Cheers!'

Harry returned the toast, though he seemed less than happy with my company. I decided to waste no time in coming to the point.

'Harry, my circumstances are less comfortable than I might have given Michael to understand.'

Harry said nothing, but it was clear from his face that he and Michael had discussed my new-found (as far as they were concerned) wealth and I suspected that they had been unenthusiastic about it.

'The fact is that while I have a certain amount of ready money, I have debts that I will need to pay by the end of the year.' I paused and composed a mournful expression. 'I fear that I will be unable to meet them.'

Harry gulped nervously at his pint, resolutely refusing to take the bait I was dangling before him.

I continued. I surprised myself at how easily the lies came. But, in the end, what was the harm? This Charlie was, I had already established from Michael's account, a blackguard of the vilest sort. If any damage was done to him, I would not mourn it. And the Home Office would hardly be concerned about Michael Radford. I told myself that I would do my childhood friend no ill and ploughed ahead with my story.

'Michael told me something of what you were doing. I have some knowledge of the world and, until my notes are due, some capital to invest in …' I paused. 'Let us say a small manufacturers.' Nothing. 'Or perhaps a little printing business.'

Now I had him. Printing was a riskier business than coining. When I had left England, counterfeiting bank notes was still punishable by death, and even now it would result in a prolonged term of imprisonment – much longer than if only coins were involved. But if one took the risk, the possibilities of gain were so much greater. Once the press was set up, paper notes could be produced quickly and each one was obviously more profitable than coin to the forger. It was common to forge notes of five or ten pounds in value, while the highest value of coin that would be forged would be a sovereign.

Harry put his drink carefully on the table and leaned closer to me. 'Do you know aught of printing?'

When I was in Borneo, we had run a small printing press to aid us in the business of governing the country. I had no personal involvement with the mechanics of the exercise, but I thought it best not to admit as much to Mr Price. Indeed, I may well have left him with the impression that I was all but an expert in the business.

Price picked up his glass, gulped at his beer, put it back on the table, fiddled with the handle, and generally displayed every possible symptom of nervousness and uncertainty. It was time, I thought, to move things on.

'Why don't you talk to Michael about the best way to move forward? I'll be in the park again tomorrow. He can find me there.'

He nodded, tipped the last of his beer down his throat, and hurried out. I watched him go and sat for a while nursing my own drink, and then, after a decent interval, set off back towards Paddington.

Things moved quickly after that. I had feared that Michael might not turn up the next day, and that I would have to visit Seven Dials again, but he was there promptly at noon. This time, knowing what I did, I noticed everybody else who came into the park. I looked suspiciously at a clergyman, a gentleman in the ubiquitous green uniform of the militia and two clerks, apparently sharing their lunchtime sandwiches. Michael noticed my nervousness, but put it down to the harsh words we had exchanged at our last meeting. He smiled reassurance and suggested that, as before, we walk as we talked. The idea that I was, in fact, not rich at all seemed to have put him at his ease with me and, for the first time, I was reminded of the companionship of our youth. We set off between the flower beds like old friends.

It never occurred to Michael to be suspicious of me. He had been open about the way in which a shortage of money had driven him to crime and now he seemed to feel a common bond with me.

'I'll see you right,' he said, 'for old times' sake.'

It was, it seemed, friendship more than any other consideration that had brought Michael to our meeting. I tried to turn the conversation to the idea that I might be able to put some money into his schemes. If he seized on such an opportunity, I could tell the Home Office that, far from having the government of France supporting them, the Seven Dials forgers were short of capital. Then, surely, the government's agents would lose interest in them. Alas, it seemed they had all the money they needed.

'For,' said Michael, 'don't we make our own?'

He was much more interested, he said, in any help I could give with printing. 'Harry says you understand the business,' he said. 'And that would be a good business to be set up in. Our problem is that getting the plate to print money is a tricky thing.'

It seemed that if they were not lacking in capital, at least nobody was supplying them with the equipment they needed. Would this, I wondered, not satisfy the Home Office? I was still convinced that, however much he might be offending against the laws of our country, Michael Radford was not the sort of man to be involved in any French plot. If I were to save him, I had to be able to convince my unwanted visitor at the hotel that Radford was a simple criminal. Once matters were in the hands of the regular police, I could escape back to Devon, taking Michael with me. Back in Bickleigh, we should both be free of this nonsense. The arm of the Metropolitan police force would not extend that far. It was only the agents of the Home Office that we had to fear.

'I might be able to help you with the plate.' God forgive me, I was drawing us all into deeper waters than Michael and his friends were already navigating, but I had to convince them that I had something to offer. Until I could demonstrate to the Home Office that there were no French spies in Seven Dials, their agents would force me to infiltrate this gang. I had to persuade Michael that it was in their interests to let me join them. The man who had forced himself upon me in my hotel had never been so crude as to make an obvious threat, but there was no doubt in my mind that he would destroy me if I did not do as he asked.

'That would be splendid!' Michael's satisfaction at my response was an arrow to my soul. Part of me wanted to warn him that he was being watched and that a trap was being set for him, but I held my tongue. I told myself that this was not just in my own interests, but in his. Surely it was best that I be the one to do the business and report that they were not traitors rather than that someone else add to the dossiers of so-called 'evidence' that had already been collected. Perhaps someone at Queen Street had once smuggled French goods. Maybe the landlord at the Crown had served them a French wine. It seemed to me that any nonsense or tittle tattle was being admitted as 'evidence' on much the same basis that the fact that the French had an army was apparently evidence that they might yet invade our country. In any case, I told myself, if I connived with the Home Office I would be in a position to know if the authorities were to move against Queen Street, and then I should have time to get Michael Radford to safety. He did not belong in Seven Dials, surrounded by vice. He belonged, I was sure, in Devon, breathing a more innocent air. Indeed, if my enforced involvement with his criminality resulted in my engineering his removal back to his true home, then surely I would be doing a good thing.

Michael was still talking, excited at the prospect of moving into a more profitable line of business, but, such was the turmoil in my heart, that I was hardly listening. Then he paused, and I realised that he had suggested that we take lunch together. 'Come on!' He was still waiting for my reply. 'It was ungracious of me to refuse you when you offered. Let us sit down and eat together today.'

I knew I should, but I could not face the idea of breaking bread with a man I might seem about to betray. Numbly, I shook my head and, muttering some excuse, made my way back to my hotel.

When I got back to my room I was scarcely surprised to discover the Home Office's agent sat there waiting for me.

'How did you get in?' I asked.

'The management are most cooperative.'

'Perhaps I should change hotel.'

I had intended the remark as a facetious response to his arrogance, but he seemed to take it at face value.

'It might be better if you took lodgings somewhere. It adds credibility to the idea that you are running out of money and looking to recover your fortunes in town.'

'I was hoping that would not be necessary.' I explained that I had met Michael – not that I needed to tell him this, because, of course, his spies had already informed him of the fact. He did not, however, know what we had spoken about. I told him the whole business of the plate. 'So you see, I am sure you are mistaken. If this were a French plot, then surely they would have been sent the plate that they needed.'

'Not necessarily. We British may not have the sort of secret police they have in France …' I allowed myself a cough at this point. Only a few days ago, I would have automatically agreed with such a statement. Now, sat opposite what was, to all intents and purposes, a secret policeman, I was somewhat more sceptical. He ignored my spluttering and continued, 'But it is less of a simple matter to smuggle printing plates into this country than you might think.'

It was as I had feared: the evidence of the plates was ignored, while the fact that the crooks were not short of capital for their enterprise was adduced to confirm that they must be receiving funding from France. Apparently, I was still to join the counterfeiting gang and inform upon them to the Home Office.

'But this is ridiculous.' I tried to reason with the man. 'I don't have any official status and, for all I know, neither have you. You have yet to tell me your name.'

'You have seen my authority.'

'It's a card, damn it.' I was angry enough to forget myself. 'Anybody can print up a card.'

'Do you seriously doubt that I am what I say I am?'

He knew all about me, he knew about the counterfeiting, he had the resources to have Michael followed. There was no doubt that he was a member of some large and official body and his sardonic smile showed that he knew that I could not seriously question his

73

credentials.

'I need a name.' I stuck to my guns. 'You are involving me in something that could be dangerous and which clearly is criminal. I need to know on whose behalf I am acting.'

'No you don't.' He was not arguing, merely stating a fact. 'When we want to contact you, we shall do so. Until then, you have only to act as we have instructed you. The less you know, the better.'

'But if I need to explain myself to the police …'

He raised his hand to silence me.

'If you get into trouble, we will do our best to help you. But if you mention our role to anybody, we will leave you to the mercies of the constabulary. We value discretion above almost all things.'

There was no more discussion. I was given my orders, still with no explicit threat, but it was clear that he considered me his creature and the power of the organisation he represented was too great for me to feel that I could sensibly choose to resist him. So I reluctantly agreed that I would move out of my comfortable room in the Royal Hotel and instead take lodgings. It was not too great a hardship, for I did not have to pretend to any extreme of poverty and after a day of discreet enquiries I was able to find myself a room in a pleasant enough house near Marylebone Lane where I had visited the police station when I started my search for Harry Price. If I had known where that search would lead, I might have left well alone, but it was too late to worry about that now.

Once I was established in my new home, I left word with Price that I would welcome a visit from Michael. He had yet to tell me his address and the omission seemed so deliberate by now that I was reluctant to ask it. I did hope, though, that an invitation to my own home might be reciprocated.

He came the day after I sent my invitation. It seemed

that a visit to my lodgings did not bother him in the way that calling on me at the hotel clearly had.

'It's a nice enough place,' he said. 'Where do you cook?'

'I don't. My landlady provides breakfast and dinner every day for sixpence.'

'You're being robbed.' He was amused, obviously enjoying the demonstration of his superiority in the economics of domestic life. 'I suppose you didn't have to cook for yourself in India.'

'No,' I admitted. 'A white man can live like a king there, with a string of servants to cook and clean.'

'You should have stayed there.'

'Ah, well.' I hesitated and then mumbled something about Cawnpore.

Michael was immediately apologetic. 'I didn't think, John. It was stupid. Forgive me.'

I forgave him easily enough, the more so as it was the first time since our argument that he had addressed me by my Christian name. Clearly the idea that I, like him, was struggling to survive in London had gone some considerable way to repairing our relationship.

Talk of my move back to England led naturally to the question of my financial condition and what might be done to improve it and thus, as I had planned, we were soon discussing the possibilities of my involving myself with his own criminal activities.

My anonymous master – for I must acknowledge that I was his man as much as the meanest servant acknowledges those in authority over him – had told me that I must make do without any plates until we knew more about the gang. Michael, of course, was all for starting a printing operation as soon as he could, but I prevaricated.

'Getting the plate will take time,' I said. 'I don't know people in London, the way I did in the East. I have to feel my way. And then we need the right paper.'

Michael nodded. I was glad that he seemed to realise that getting watermarked paper would be the most difficult part of the exercise. It suggested that he had given the matter some thought and understood his business.

'Why don't you show me how you are working things now?' I said. 'I may have some thoughts as to how things can be improved or, at any rate, there may be some area in which I can make myself useful.'

'There might indeed.' Michael allowed himself a broad and totally genuine smile. 'I have a notion that there is something you could do for us.'

I obviously asked to know what that might be, but he would not answer. 'I'll let it be a surprise,' he said. 'In any case, I had best ask Charlie first, before we make any definite decision.'

'Ah, yes, the famous Mr Charlie. Does he have any other name?'

Michael looked sharply up at me and I cursed myself for my stupidity. 'Charlie not good enough for you?'

I was quick to reassure him that Charlie's surname was nothing to me. This was, indeed, the case, the Home Office having already provided me with that information. I had asked simply to give myself a better idea of the relationship between Michael and Charlie and how much confidence there was between them.

I tried a different tack. 'I was only surprised that you seem so comfortable with him when he led such a cruel attack upon your friend.'

'Yes, well …' Michael hesitated and then, to my surprise, seemed to try to exculpate this Charlie from responsibility for his friend's distress. 'That was by way of business. There was no malice in it. And he struck no blows himself.'

I think it was that last phrase that made me realise the nature of the world that I had found myself in: a world where a man might stand and watch his victim beaten but be acclaimed blameless if he had 'struck no blows himself'. Life, it seemed, must be held quite cheap if this was the morality that governed men's affairs. I thought, for the first time, of the danger that I might have put myself into. If my role as a spy – for surely that is what I was – were to be discovered, would Michael do away with me and insist that 'there was no malice in it'? Would he stand by and tell himself afterwards that he had 'struck no blows himself'? It seemed to me that such violence combined with such sophistry made the inhabitants of Seven Dials more savage than any Dyak taking heads in the jungles of Borneo. Was this the vaunted 'Civilisation' that Britain was carrying to the farthest corners of the Earth?

It was clear to me then, if it had not been before, that I must tread carefully and I took care that I did not betray my horror to Michael. Instead, I sipped my tea and feigned attention as he explained more about the mechanics of coining.

Despite my efforts, I found it difficult to concentrate on what he told me at that meeting. Fortunately, though, his enthusiasm for his new trade was such that he always welcomed the opportunity to talk about it. So, when Charlie had been duly consulted and I was officially introduced to the business, he saw nothing odd in his having to explain it all again. Indeed, it was clear that he would have explained it all again anyway.

It was a week or so after he had called on me in my lodgings when I made my first visit to what I suppose can best be referred to as 'the coiners' den'. I made my way to Queen Street as before. This time I was wearing clothes that I had bought since I was in London: an outfit that drew less attention in that part of town. It was still respectable but my top hat had been replaced with a billycock, my trousers and waistcoat were of corduroy and my shirt was of a coarser fabric. I had avoided second-hand clothes, as I had no facilities to boil-wash them and no desire to share the fleas and lice of the previous owner – assuming that fleas and lice were the worst that might be passed on to me. I had heard too many cases of people dying from diseases acquired from second-hand clothes for me to feel that this was a risk worth taking. When it came to the shoes, however, I decided that second-hand would have to do. New clothes were not that conspicuous after a few days of wear and could easily enough be explained by a burst of good fortune, but shoes in Seven Dials were precious items to be used until the soles were utterly worn through. New shoes would immediately make me conspicuous and would lead to comment on my apparent wealth. My shoes, I decided, must be old and purchased from the meanest of slop houses. Fortunately I found a pair that were both sound and comfortable. Indeed, the leather, softened from use, moulded itself to my feet better than the pair that I had paid good money for in Plymouth.

I was conscious of the feel of the cobbles through the worn soles of my 'new' footwear as I walked the by now familiar street. As the place was no longer strange to me, so I was no longer a stranger to the inhabitants, who scarcely cast a glance as I passed by. On my arrival at the house, the giant did not accost me, but, opening a door beneath the stairs, shouted, 'Michael!'

Michael Radford appeared a few moments later and, bounding into the hall with an enthusiasm I had not seen him express before, seized my hand and shook it vigorously.

'It's good to see you.' He started down the stairs to the cellar, still shaking my hand, which had the effect of pulling me with him. Laughing, as he realised what he was doing, he released me but beckoned that I should follow.

The cellars had clearly been intended for storage and there was no natural light down there. The glow of oil lamps allowed me to make out a large space with people bent to some invisible task at their work-benches, but it was not until my eyes had adjusted to the gloom that I was able to gain any clear impression of what they were doing.

There seemed to be a veritable factory in that gloom, manufacturing coins on an almost industrial scale. On one work-bench the glow of a small brazier illuminated the face of a man stirring a pot, which bubbled in the flames. As I watched a child passed us and gave a handful of small objects to the man who examined them critically and added them to his mixture.

'Put young Jeb down for tuppence,' he called across to where, under the illumination provided by one of the lamps, an elderly figure scratched at what looked like the sort of account book I used to keep in Borneo.

I could hear the tap of metal on metal and the rasp of files, the meaning of which was immediately obvious to me. Less easily explained were the flashes of white light that every so often broke the gloom, almost as if lightning was striking inside the cellar.

The air was foul with the stench of bodies – few of which appeared over-concerned with cleanliness – the smell of the oil lamps and whatever was being burnt under that brazier. There was, too, that metallic tang that attends any sort of foundry and, underlying all the other odours, a whiff of the ocean, which I could not explain.

I coughed and put a handkerchief to my face. Michael grinned, his teeth (he had very good teeth) white against the prevailing gloom. 'I'm planning to put some ventilation in.' He gestured to where a patch of deeper darkness in the gloom betokened the presence of an old coal chute. 'We'll put a grating at the top of the chute and rig a fan to draw in good air. I'm not sure, though, how we'll keep the fan turning.'

'You need a *punkahwallah*.'

I had spoken without thought, intending the remark as a joke, but Michael asked what I meant and I explained how the fans in India had been turned by the continual motion of a man who pulled repeatedly on a rope which, by a system of pulleys, kept the fan moving.

'Aye, that would work,' he said, and insisted that I sketch out details of the arrangement. Fortunately, my time as a sailor had given me a good eye for any run of ropes and pulleys, these being almost at the core of a sailor's life, so I was able to draw from memory a system that I judged would work well enough.

'But,' I pointed out, 'the system demands a person to operate it.' In Cawnpore, most homes had two *punkahwallahs* who took turns to sit pulling at the rope for as long as their master remained in the room, so as to ensure that the white man's delicate constitution would be spared the still, hot air of the Indian summer. Even though I was assured that the arrangement was hallowed by custom and that it would draw critical attention from my neighbours if I did not hire men to operate my *punkahs*, I was always uncomfortable with the system. The unfortunate *punkahwallah* must sit for hours performing his monotonous task and I thought of the stories of the despots of ancient Rome fanned by slaves and it seemed that I offered my servant little more than modern slavery. The reality of life in India, though, was that the natives had little option but to take what work they could find, however demeaning and poorly rewarded. But in England, even in Seven Dials, there were surely no white men who would consent to perform such a task.

Michael, as I explained my concerns, could scarce forbear from laughing out loud. 'I shall rig up this system and offer sixpence a day to any boy who will consent to operate it, and I will be hard put to beat off the mob that will descend on me demanding employment.'

And so, within minutes of arriving to look over Michael's place of work I had my first lesson in the reality of employment in Seven Dials. It was, for me, a sobering experience but, if my discomfort showed on my face, Michael did not notice it. 'You see,' he said, flourishing my sketch, 'not here five minutes and already you're making improvements about the place.' He grasped my hand and drew me to him in a clumsy embrace. 'I'm glad you found me. This is our future, John. We're going to be rich.'

Michael showed me every detail of his workshop, asking me all the time if I had any ideas for improvements. After the business of the fan, he seemed convinced that I was some sort of mechanical genius and that I would have insights into all the elements of his operation, but I could see little that was not already terrifyingly efficient.

The brazier was melting metal – the raw material of the new coinage. 'Britannia metal spoons are best,' Michael said. 'The kids steal them from coffee houses and such and we pay them a ha'penny apiece. We try to be fair though. If they bring us a silver spoon – and it's been known to happen, for some of the children are not that bright – then we'll give them a threepenny piece. I always make it the thruppence and not three pennies for they do get excited by the silver coin. We give them real ones, mind. None of the tin.' As he spoke, one of his little thieves happened to be passing and he reached out and ruffled the lad's hair with apparently genuine affection. 'Children are still children, even if they live in this hell-hole,' he said.

From the brazier, the molten metal was ladled into plaster moulds. 'These are the ones that we got when we took over the business. We're making our own now, but they're devilishly fiddly.'

He showed me some coins fresh from the moulds and they did, indeed, bear a passing good resemblance to the originals, though the colour was wrong – they had a bluish sheen, quite unlike the silver they were supposed to counterfeit. 'We file around the edges to take off any imperfections. Then comes the magic bit.'

He led me past the bench where the coins were being made at what seemed to me a furious rate. A minute after separating the moulds to produce one batch of false coins – and I say 'batch' as each mould produced four coins at a time – they were being refilled with molten metal, so that a large basin was being steadily filled with false shillings.

'This is where we coat the tin with silver.' Michael gestured to where, on the next bench, a great glass jar stood with metal plates submerged in some clear liquid. I went towards it to look more closely in the gloom of the cellar, but Michael put a restraining hand upon my shoulder. 'Don't get too close. If you were to splash any of it on your skin, it would burn terribly.' It was, he explained, a mixture of nitric and sulphuric acid. 'It is what we call a galvanic battery,' he said. 'It passes an electric current. Mr Faraday tells us that one day it will be used for all manner of things, but for now we use it to coat the base metal with real silver.' He pointed to a glass dish with a little liquid in it, where one of the false shillings lay connected to a wire that ran from his battery. He reached towards this wire, disturbing the apparatus and there was a sudden flash of light and that strange smell – one that I associated with hot days at sea – was suddenly strong within the basement, though we were a fair stretch from the river.

'Ooops!' He laughed, apparently regarding the accident as of little consequence. 'You have to take care with these things.'

He bent to the wire again and, having removed it from the dish, he extracted the coin with a pair of tongs and held it towards me. The bluish tinge was quite gone: instead the coin shone brightly silver.

'It's a work of art,' Michael said. 'It's a shame to spoil it but we'll dirty it up before we send it out. A coin as shiny as that will attract suspicion.

I looked around the cellar.

'And all these people are producing shillings?'

'No, the shillings were just the start. I told you that we made our own moulds now. You have to be careful, but the principle is easy enough. You take an impression of the coin in plaster of Paris and there's your mould.'

He moved on to the next bench. 'These are florins and over there are half-crowns. You can only make those two at a time, because the weight of metal means the moulds get too hot and crack if you try to mould four at a time like with the shillings.'

'I'd have thought the shillings scarcely worth the trouble.'

Michael shook his head. 'The shillings are our bread and butter, John. Remember that the trickiest part of the whole process is passing the coins. Shillings are easily passed. There is less call for florins and half-crowns and they are more carefully examined. Besides' – and here came that grin again – 'we make a prodigious quantity of tin here and it's best that it's not all the same denomination or it becomes a little too obvious.'

It was a wise precaution, but the forgers had not been careful enough. I would have warned him, but I knew it was already too late.

'But you are right, John, to say that we would make more money out of the more valuable coins. And that's why we are expanding our work.'

By now, we were in the very farthest reach of the cellar and it was so dark I was having trouble in seeing. Despite this, one corner was separated from the rest by a sort of screen or curtain of sacking. We now passed behind this, where three men were hunched over more moulds and another of the galvanic batteries.

'This,' and Michael had dropped his voice close to a whisper, 'is our greatest enterprise.'

One oil lamp on the wall, with a metal reflector behind

it, provided just enough light to see by. Michael went over to the glass bowl beside the galvanic battery. Unlike the ones in the rest of the cellar, this one had a small spirit burner beneath it to keep it warm.

'And here we are,' he said. 'Our piece de resistance.' He pronounced the words in the English fashion, having presumably seen them written without having heard them in French. It was a reassuring reminder of Michael Radford the Devon man, who seemed to be almost subsumed into the character of Michael Radford the master criminal.

I looked into the final dish and saw, to my amazement, what I took to be a golden sovereign.

'That looks about ready, Joseph.' Michael was addressing a young man who sat perched on a stool watching the apparatus much as a head clerk watched over the lines of writers in an office.

The young man leaned forward and looked critically at the coin. 'I'd give it another minute or two, Mr Radford.'

Michael nodded and turned to me. 'Joseph's a good lad. He has an eye for his work.'

I was still trying to take in all that I had seen. I did not know if I was more staggered by the scale of the enterprise – for this was a factory, not just a workshop – or the respect accorded to my childhood friend, or the sophistication of the techniques employed.

Michael was watching me, clearly waiting for some response.

'How did this Joseph learn such skills?' It was the first question I could think of to ask and, perhaps, a foolish one, for a flicker of irritation showed on Michael's face before he replied with a smile.

'I taught him, John.'

'But how …?'

'How could a poor ignorant farm hand know these things?'

I stood tongue-tied, for that, indeed, had been my thought.

'Let's get upstairs and we'll talk.'

He guided me back towards the steps and we climbed up to the hallway again. I glanced back before he shut the door. Below, I saw figures move in the gloom, illuminated by flashes of electric light. The stink seemed to have ascended with me. As I watched, someone must have added fuel to the brazier, for there was a flicker of flame. The picture reminded me of the images of hell that had been drummed into me in Sunday school. It was the realm of the damned, where those whom God had cast down filled their days with sin. And here next to me was Michael, who appeared Lord of that domain.

'Come on.' The man I had just, in my mind, characterised as Satan was smiling at me. 'Let's get ourselves a cup of tea.'

I suppose I should not have been surprised by what happened next, but I was. You must remember that I had not been aware of my own nature until my time with Mr Brooke in Borneo. I knew, of course, that there were sodomites in England. Everyone knew. But everyone pretended that such men were exceptional creatures. Indeed, every now and then one would be taken up and charged with his unnatural crimes and might find himself hanged by the neck as a proper punishment for such vice. The idea, then, that any of those I knew might share my predilections had seemed fantastical. Oh, yes, in the small hours of the night when I lay alone in bed wondering if I might ever find love again, then I might have fancied that this or that person might share my feelings and, if I am to be wholly honest, Michael's visage may have sometimes featured in such nocturnal fantasies. But awake, walking the respectable streets of Queen Victoria's respectable London, I knew such things to be impossible.

Only we were not in respectable London now. We were in Seven Dials.

We climbed the stairs. I stepped over the missing treads automatically.

One floor up, we stepped towards a familiar door.

'That's Harry Price's room.'

Michael turned, a half-smile on his face. 'You hadn't realised?'

And at that moment I did realise and things that had made no sense to me were suddenly blindingly obvious.

Harry Price opened the door to us and greeted his friend with a radiant smile and then, turning to me, he shook my hand. 'I didn't want to tell you, but Michael said you would be all right.' It was all he said on the matter.

Michael and I sat on the two chairs while Harry fussed about and made us tea – no small exercise, for there was no stove in the room and he had to vanish away to find hot water. 'There's a communal kitchen,' Michael explained. 'It's not ideal but Rome wasn't built in a day.'

The tea, when it appeared, was served up in cups that might well have been used in the heyday of the house: fine china with a gold rim. On matching plates were almond cakes. 'From the baker's down the road,' Harry said. 'We may not be Belgravia, but we do have wonderful cakes.' Harry sat on the bed, while Michael and I sipped and nibbled with enthusiasm and, I had to admit, it was as fine a tea as I ever took at the Royal Hotel and a good deal better than anything my current landlady would have provided.

Between bites of almond cake Michael explained how he had become so well-informed about the practicalities of his new employment. 'You must remember that I came to London with the firm intention of improving myself. The occupation that I now find myself engaged in was not, it is true, the sort of work that I had anticipated, but I saw no reason why I should give up my hopes of self-improvement.' To this end, Michael had enrolled for lectures at the Mechanics Institute. This had involved an element of deception, as the Institute had been established for the benefit of respectable artisans and it is doubtful if even the most liberal interpretation of the same could stretch to his employment. However, a mind that took so naturally to forging coin of the realm was hardly likely to be foiled by its inability to obtain a ticket to the lectures legitimately.

The Institute had been set up specifically to benefit men like Michael – men whose station in life meant they had no proper education although their minds were as sharp as any gentleman's. He took naturally to the lectures. 'They made things so clear,' he said. 'Great men came from the universities to share their knowledge with us.' The lectures were exclusively on scientific and technical subjects, and, in the discussions which frequently followed the classes, Michael soon distinguished himself as one of the abler students. He took to extending his studies and became a frequent reader at the Institute's library. Although he had started with a simple desire, like so many of his class, to gain an education for its own sake, he soon realised that many of the techniques that he was learning could be applied to any form of manufacturing. I was scarcely surprised to learn that this was so, for I had heard great things of Dr Birkbeck's social experiment, which had been designed specifically to enable working men to contribute to that excellence in engineering and the sciences which underpins the greatness of Britain. The good doctor would, of course, have been horrified had he known that his efforts had been put to work to improve the manufacturing not of machinery or trade goods but of illicit currency.

Michael settled his cup neatly back onto the table. 'You need hardly be surprised that I have gained an education. As I recall, you could neither read nor write when you left Bickleigh.'

He was right, of course. We were both, in our different ways, examples of how modern Britain allowed its sons to rise from humble origins by the exercise of talent. Yet, starting in the same small village, how differently our lives had turned out.

I looked at Michael, as assured in his administration of Sir Charles Crawley's criminal empire as I had been running Sarawak for James Brooke or assisting the Collector in Cawnpore. Perhaps our lives had not turned out so differently in the end. After all, we were both together now, sitting in the same room in an abandoned property in a foul slum, planning our joint enterprise in criminality.

Michael, having explained his education, was moving on to practical issues about the development of his operation. 'You've arrived at just the right moment, John. We can't do much more with silver. We need to move on to gold. As ever, the problem is passing it out and, obviously, that problem is much greater with sovereigns than with half-crowns. People are careful with sovereigns. They bite at them, thinking to tell if the coin is a true gold alloy or softer lead. Most will be unable to judge the difference, but some will, and, in any case, there's always a danger they'll bite through the plating, for that really is gold and we keep it very thin.'

He took another sip of his tea and passed me an almond cake. 'Our biggest problem, though, is that we don't look like men who would have sovereigns honestly come by on their person. If we are going to shift a quantity of them – and I do intend to shift a goodly number – then we need someone who looks like a gentleman. And that's where you come in. You can play the part of a toff who can spend them in the sort of shops that would never take a bad coin from the likes of me. You're a gift from the gods, you are, John. The Jew-shops in Hatton Garden will not allow the likes of us in, but you will get served and they won't think to test your coin, for they see less tin there than the poor folk.'

I was not happy at the idea of being so directly involved in robbing the public, for once the forgeries were discovered, the loss would fall on those who had taken them. I was also aware that it was the individuals who passed out the false coinage who were the most likely to be taken up by the constables. Yet I could not fault Michael's logic. There were no obvious improvements to be made in his workshop and there were no tasks carried out down there which could not be done as well, or better, by those already engaged in their felonious trade. And if I did not undertake to swindle the shopkeepers, some other man would be found eventually. Besides, it was hardly as if the jewellers of Hatton Garden could not afford a few sovereigns. So, after the briefest of pauses, I nodded my agreement.

'Don't worry, John. You won't be spending all your time passing out tin. You'll have time to talk to printers and establish what we will need to move into the printing of currency notes.'

I forced a smile. Printing currency would move us into still murkier waters and my mysterious friend from the Home Office might decide to pounce. I had no wish to be the means by which the authorities brought Michael – or Harry Price for that matter – before the Courts, yet I could see no way out of the snares that the Home Office had laid for me. I could not flee back to Devon, for the authorities clearly knew all about me and would easily apprehend me in Bickleigh. My best chance was to find some evidence against Charles Crawley and hope that if the police captured him, then Michael might escape. But so far, I had yet to meet Sir Charles.

'Have another almond cake.' Michael passed me the plate with the last one. I declined it politely, but he insisted. 'We can afford it.' He grinned. 'We're going to be rich.'

I took the cake and nibbled at it. It should have been delicious, but it was all I could do to swallow it down.

CHAPTER SIX

I started on what I suppose I should call my life of crime the next day. As Michael said, there was nothing to gain by delay: he already had a stock of 'golden' sovereigns that he was anxious to dispose of.

Michael's idea that I should simply patronise some Bond Street jeweller and there convert my forged money into marketable produce was not as straightforward as he seemed to think. Not being in a condition of life to have familiarity with such places, Michael had rather assumed that, as when Harry had bought the almond cakes, my transaction would naturally involve a transfer of cash. I had to disabuse him: when gentlemen go shopping for expensive gee-gaws, the business is generally done on account, with the goods (and the bill) delivered to the gentleman's abode. Of course, if I were to say that I wanted to take the jewellery with me, a cash payment would be expected, but the transaction would be sufficiently unusual for the jeweller to pay it careful attention, which was the last thing that we wanted.

In the end, we came up with a subterfuge which I was reasonably confident would work. We commissioned the assistance of a young woman named Susan, who had arrived in London from Bicester some months previously and fallen into a life of vice. 'She's a nice enough girl,' Michael assured me. 'She's not really cut out for this life, so she'll be glad enough of the change.'

Susan, when I met her, did indeed seem a nice enough girl. Her father had been a baker, but on his decease ('Just upped and died,' she told me, 'on a Tuesday, just after he opened the shop.') her mother had been unable to make the place pay. The family had got into debt and Susan had left for the metropolis in the hope of repairing her fortunes, but, like so many other young girls, she had fallen in with bad company and, being desperate for money and having no reputation left to preserve, she had turned to selling her body to survive.

Susan still had a little of the bloom of the country on her, though she was already developing a certain hardness in her features which seems common to women who make their money as she did. Still, once Michael and I had dressed her up in clothes that we purchased especially for the business at hand, she could pass as respectable.

Our first foray was made that afternoon to the Burlington Arcade. Michael assured me that my companion's appearance would be entirely unremarked there. So, having dressed myself in my smartest suit, I repaired to Piccadilly with her on my arm.

Despite the new outfit, the girl could not but look what she was and anyone watching our progress through the West End would see a gentleman with his poll. This was a role that, given my nature, was one that I had never played before. I must admit that, in anticipation, I had believed that I would be mortified with embarrassment, and was uncertain that I would be able to pull it off, but, in the event, I found myself but one of many promenading with a woman clearly not my wife. Indeed, once I had opened my eyes to what was going on around me, it seemed that the Burlington Arcade was as rife with vice as Seven Dials – but in the Arcade the women were much better dressed and the signs of pox less immediately visible.

Accompanied by this woman, it seemed natural that we would find ourselves loitering in front of a jeweller's window. She pointed enthusiastically at the display, while I made as if I were anxious to be off down the street. Once I was sure that our dumb show had been noticed by the staff inside the shop – one of whom, I could swear, was trying unsuccessfully to hide his smile – I shrugged resignedly and went in alone, pointedly leaving my companion outside. With every appearance of embarrassment and awkwardness, which required little in the way of acting on my part, I indicated that I wanted a small bracelet from the window display. I had carefully chosen an item that might reasonably be purchased with ready money. The assistant picked it from the window and, without being asked, made it up into a neatly wrapped packet.

'Sir will be taking his purchase with him?' he asked, struggling to conceal his smirk.

I nodded, blushing.

'That will be three guineas, sir.'

I reached into my pocket and withdrew three golden coins and three (real) shillings, which I slapped onto the counter, grabbing at my parcel and heading towards the door. The assistant was clearly amused and watched as I hastened towards my lady friend and passed her the package. She immediately threw her arms around me and, from the corner of my eye, I saw the shopman, his eyes glued to this indecorous display, toss the coins into a drawer without any proper examination at all.

We moved a little further down the Arcade, until we were out of sight of anyone in the first shop, and repeated the procedure. This time, the assistant did pick up the first coin to inspect it. Susan, feigning impatience, rapped sharply on the window and the assistant took pity on me and hurried to hand over my parcel. The forgery was well up to passing that sort of examination. Indeed, in the four shops we visited in the course of the afternoon, only in one did the staff give my coinage more than a passing glance and, even then, my apparent respectability – leaving aside the question of the company I was keeping – seemed to encourage them to accept the coin as what it claimed to be.

Buoyed by the success of our first day's efforts, we moved on to Bond Street. Susan's appearance was a little more conspicuous there, as it was not so well known an area for women of her type as was the Burlington Arcade. Even so, Susan was not the only professional woman to be out with her gentleman friend and we were able to repeat the charade of the previous day with some success.

Michael was well pleased with our haul and we were encouraged to put on a similar performance in Hatton Garden the next day. This proved a mistake. The jewellers of Hatton Garden do not just retail, but actually produce, their goods, and the little Jew who took my sovereigns obviously handled gold often enough to detect something amiss. My apparently respectable demeanour would not save me. I could claim that one bad coin had been passed to me and I was an innocent victim, but three would lead to the calling of a constable. My appearance, though, was such that the Jew did not immediately call for the doors to be locked. I saw him look carefully at the coin and toss it lightly in his hand, measuring its weight. I did not hesitate but made immediately for the door and ran off down the street. Fortunately, the girl had recognised the danger even before I had and was already well away from the shop by the time the staff emerged in pursuit.

Although I had a decent start on my pursuers, I was no longer a young man and I had little hope of escape. I had, though, reckoned without the feelings of the costermongers whose cries as they hawked their wares were a familiar background to life in this part of town. They made a precarious living, perched uneasily on the divide between legitimate traders and purveyors of stolen goods. Although they were just trying to survive, they faced continual persecution from the police and when more respectable traders, who were always trying to get the costermongers moved on, set up a hue and cry, they would naturally take the part of the hunted rather than the hunters. It must be said, too, that their sympathies were seldom with those of the Hebraic persuasion.

As I darted past one barrow, a foot was put out behind me and the first of my pursuers went sprawling. He was foolish enough to turn on the man who had tripped him – a big brute I suspected I had seen about Seven Dials. The altercation that ensued was short and ended with the shopman and two of his colleagues nursing broken noses and the costermonger wheeling his barrow along the lane whistling as if he had not a care in the world. I saw this, as can be imagined, from a distance, and slowed my pace, but it seemed wiser not to remain in the vicinity and, shortly after, I returned to Seven Dials to report my failure.

Michael, it transpired, already knew of my misfortune. There was little that happened within a mile of Queen Street of which he was not almost immediately cognisant. He was sanguine about the loss of three coins. 'We have plenty more and your efforts yesterday exceeded all our expectations.' He accepted, though, that I was in no condition to make any more efforts at passing coins today. In any case, my 'lady-friend' had not yet returned. Instead, he suggested that I should turn my mind to the question of setting up a press.

Printing the notes, I thought, should be simple enough: the problem was, of course, to obtain the plates from which the prints would be made, and then to find appropriate paper (for the Bank of England issued notes on watermarked paper which would be near impossible to forge).

There seemed no possibility of obtaining genuine plates. I would have to find someone who could engrave them, copying from a bank note.

London, capital of an Empire on which the sun never sets, is home to every sort of artisan, but how, I wondered, would I find someone who would undertake work so clearly illegal and punishable by a considerable period of imprisonment or even transportation? When I shared my concern with Michael, he simply laughed. 'Search among the bankrupts,' he said, and moved on to supervise the work of some new arrival in the cellar.

The idea of bankruptcy was, of course, entirely familiar to me. Even in India – where conditions made it difficult for a European to fail entirely – there were merchants whose businesses crashed, usually because of some disaster, such as a warehouse fire or the loss of goods at sea. In England, I could not be unaware of the gossip about the failure of great lords to meet their debts. Their ruin might be because of unwary speculation, but more often because of gambling and excess. Their cases would be written of in the newspapers and were a source of innocent entertainment at all levels of society. There is nothing, after all, that people enjoy more than to see their betters reduced in their station. What I had not realised, though, was the degree to which business failure was endemic in the artisan class. Every year, it seemed, a thousand printers would establish themselves in London and, every year, half of them would fail. A great man loses his money and the printer he had commissioned to produce his book of verse is not paid; a railway speculator is declared bankrupt and the man who printed his prospectus is condemned to poverty alongside him. London is full of those who have taken up the challenge of this modern age and raised themselves from poverty to comfort, and we all take note of them. We are less likely to notice those who have come to the city and, through bad luck or poor judgement, have failed utterly and find themselves reduced to the condition of those who inhabit the rookeries.

I started my search in the public houses near the City. It was an area, or so I had been told, that has always been home to many in the printing trade. They are easily identified: the ink stains their fingers and all the washing in the world never seems to quite clean them.

For the outlay of a few hours and the price of half-a-dozen drinks, I found myself seated alongside several men with years of experience in the print. Like most artisans when gathered together in a group, the talk turned naturally to others in their trade and, as is equally natural, the gossip flowed more readily when they talked about absent friends. The gentlest of questioning provided the names of half-a-dozen men whose businesses had failed.

Another round of drinks resulted in some indiscreet comments about the reasons for their failure. Those whose businesses had collapsed because of shoddy work were of no interest to me. That ruled out half of them. Of the rest, only one remained in London, the others having retreated to lick their wounds elsewhere.

I might have heard of the one that was still in London, I tell them, as I order another round. Did fine engraving work, didn't he? No: the others are definite. Samuel could set a line of type faster than anyone, but he never touched engraved work. Didn't do it himself, didn't have a man who did it for him.

I drank with them for a while longer. It seemed polite and the beer was good, but I had no further interest in their conversation.

The next day, despite my protestations, Michael had me out changing money again. There was no question of going back to Hatton Garden and I might be remembered if I returned to Burlington Arcade or Bond Street. We decided that I should try my luck at one of the department stores. Marshall and Snelgrove was no longer new (though the very idea of such a place was new to me), but it still attracted crowds who were excited by such a different approach to shopping. In such a crowd, I hoped to be more inconspicuous. The numbers of customers might also mean that the assistants would have less time to check the coin they were offered.

Again, I was accompanied by young Susan, though we were not to play the same roles. Having a companion, I felt, made it easier for me to linger, choosing moments when the counter was busier and always approaching the youngest and least experienced of the staff.

I needed to buy items that were portable and could easily be resold. Marshall and Snelgrove was not an ideal starting point: they dealt mainly in clothing and furniture. They did, though, carry a nice selection of pens and I purchased two; one plainly masculine, and the other decorated with cloisonné work, which I presented to my companion. I offered to pay with a banknote for five pounds, which led to the supervisor being called for and a degree of excitement. I then recalled that I had a sovereign somewhere and, after fussing at one pocket and then another, I at last triumphantly withdrew the coin. By now, there were other customers waiting to be served and the staff clearly felt that more than enough time had been allocated to my purchase. The sovereign was passed into the cash register with barely a glance and we withdrew with our pens and a couple of shillings in change.

We dared not try the same trick again in Marshall and Snelgrove, for I had noticed that the establishment employed store walkers who merged with the customers to keep an eye out for potential thieves. If we were to repeat our performance in another department, I suspected there was rather too much chance of detection. Nonetheless, we had a successful day moving from shop to shop throughout the West End. After a while, I stopped buying more expensive items and started to purchase cheaper things, less interested in the items themselves than the honest coin we were given in change when all we could proffer was a sovereign.

It is a peculiarity of human nature that it is easier for someone with the appearance of a gentleman to swindle you out of three sovereigns than out of a smaller sum. The men and women who sell luxury goods to the gentry are used to dealing in gold and take it almost for granted. When, though, you offer a sovereign for some trifle worth a few shillings, then your coin is examined with care. It was Susan, who had clearly had her own experience of passing false money, who taught me the way to go about it.

'What you do,' she said, clearly relishing her role as my instructor, 'is you offer the fella in the shop a real coin – that's a sovereign for you.' A certain wistfulness in her voice suggested that she was used to using this trick for much smaller coins. 'Anyway, you offers him the sovereign and he'll be suspicious, because you don't have anything smaller, but he looks at the coin, checks it's good and goes to put it in the till. Just before he does, you say, "Oh, I think I have the right change after all." He gives you back the sovereign and you mess around with some silver, but discover – oh dear – you don't have the right money. You give him back the sovereign and he puts it in the till. Only, of course, it isn't the same sovereign.'

She smiled, obviously proud of her cunning. I could not share her enthusiasm for swindling these small shopkeepers, but I really had no choice, and her tactic proved surprisingly successful. Indeed, Harry seemed very approving of our day's haul when I handed it over to him that evening – Michael apparently being out about some other business.

'He'll be happy with this,' he said.

Harry had become much more relaxed around me since Michael had admitted me into the secret of their living arrangements. Did he recognise a clandestine brotherhood? I did not know. I certainly had no intention of volunteering any information as to my own proclivities.

'Is Michael at the Mechanics Institute?'

'No.' Harry's face suddenly closed up, as it had when he was concealing his relationship with Michael. 'He's at one of his other meetings.'

I did not probe. Clearly, I was not the only one at Queen Street who had secrets.

My secret life was waiting for me when I got back to my lodgings.

'How did you get in?'

I should have been surprised or angry or both, but it is a measure of the power he had established over me that my response was just this petulant query.

'Your landlady was ... cooperative,' he said. He never explained and I never spoke to my landlady of the matter. My tormentor and his little card with the Home Secretary's signature seemed to possess such power that it was easier not to think too hard about what he might be capable of. Certainly, suborning a landlady would be a trivial matter to him. 'I find that people are usually cooperative. They want to help. Like you, for instance.' There was the slightest of pauses and, when I did not immediately respond he prompted, 'You have news for me.'

It was a statement, not a question.

'There is no news.'

He was sitting on my only chair while I stood before him like a recalcitrant schoolboy. Now he steepled his fingers.

'You can do better than that, Williamson.'

I stepped back. The bed was behind me and I sat, trying to think of something that would convince him that neither Radford nor I could be of any interest to him.

'They are forgers,' I said. 'But that is all they are.' I tried to keep the desperation out of my voice while he looked at me quizzically over his fingers. 'There is no French plot. They are forgers, pure and simple.'

'They are forgers, indeed. But neither pure nor simple.' He cocked his head and looked at me, rather like a thrush examining a particularly juicy worm. 'Do you know where your friend' – he gave the word 'friend' an unpleasant tone – 'is spending his evening?'

I shook my head. 'I'm sure you're going to tell me.'

That look again. 'No. No, I think you should ask him yourself. And then you should turn your mind to finding out how we can get Sir Charles Crawley indicted for treason.' He rose to his feet, and started towards the door. With his hand on the doorknob, he turned.

'After all, if we can't get Sir Charles we will just have to content ourselves with Radford and your other ragamuffin chums. There's always a danger, I suppose, that you might get caught up with them.'

And then he opened the door, and was gone.

I took to my bed. I could not face my landlady, or the shabby-genteel dining room where she served up her over-cooked pork chops and, on Friday, sad fillets of cod. There were two fellow lodgers – clerks in some city firm, off to their employment before eight in the morning and often home barely in time for our seven o'clock evening meal. They would sit to dinner, their fingers stained with ink, and their conversation would be limited to cricket. Had my nemesis spoken with them? Were my views on the national game to be examined by the Home Office for evidence of my patriotic fervour or lack thereof? I had never been interested in cricket, but now I wondered if that might end up being used as evidence that I was not a loyal subject of the Queen.

It was all ridiculous, I knew, but no more ridiculous than the way that I had suddenly become embroiled in a situation utterly beyond my experience.

As I lay there, trying to think of some way out of the circumstances I found myself trapped in, I realised how lonely I was. I had been alone, really, all my life, except those brief interludes with James Brooke and Mungo Buksh. Now, back in England after so long away, I knew no one. I suppose I had hoped that Michael Radford might be a friend to me. I thought of the insinuation that my visitor had put into the word 'friend' and felt a twist in my stomach. Were such as I to be denied any friendship in case it turned to love? But, there again, was my friendship for Michael pure? Did I not, perhaps, think over-much of his virile body, his deep blue eyes?

I lay awake, plagued by black thoughts. I imagined Michael safe in bed with Harry and, for a moment, I hated Harry for having that which I now believed would ever be denied to me.

My landlady knocked on the door. Would I not be eating? No, I replied from my bed, I was unwell.

I heard her moving away. Now that I had been reminded of it, the thought of food made me suddenly hungry, but I could not go down to dinner now.

Outside, it was still light. I heard the sound of horses' hoofs striking against the cobbles and the rumble of wheels as carts passed the house. There were children playing in the street. There was laughter and companionship and happiness out there and I lay wretched and alone in my narrow bed. No wonder I had ended up spending my days in Seven Dials: that was where I belonged, wallowing in filth with the outcasts of the world.

Eventually I slept and woke the next morning with a vague remembrance of dreams filled with darkness and horror. Some of this must have shown on my face, for at breakfast my landlady asked if I was not still ill and suggested that she might recommend a doctor. I assured her that I was sufficiently recovered and, after I had eaten my dried haddock and washed it down with a cup of milky tea, I set off for another day's work at Seven Dials.

Michael greeted me cheerfully. He was, as Harry had predicted, well pleased with my previous day's work.

'There is no shortage of stores on Oxford Street,' he said. 'You and Susan make a good team. I think you should go out again today.'

'What about looking for a printer?'

He was in the room he shared with Harry and busy with some papers on the table. He had already returned his attention to them, but, at my question, he looked up. 'You've been asking around in public houses, haven't you?'

I nodded.

'Well, you're better doing that later in the day. I'll tell you what: work until lunchtime and then take Susan for a nice meal out. You both deserve it and you can pay with tin.' He turned back to his papers and I moved to the door. As I was opening it, he added, 'Get plenty of change,' and grinned.

Only as I was on my way down the stairs did I remember that I had meant to ask him where he had gone last night.

I can think of nothing of interest to say about that morning. We visited half-a-dozen shops and passed half-a-dozen sovereigns. Criminal work, like any other sort of work, becomes mechanical and dull. There is an element of risk, of course, but less so than in many other forms of employment. In any case, familiarity soon takes the edge off the danger. There is danger simply being out on the street. After less than a month in London, I had already seen the body of a man crushed by a runaway cart. It happens all the time: the horses are frightened by a sudden noise, a dog playfully nips at their legs, or they slip as the cart pulls downhill and, panicking, gather their legs beneath them and bolt. The crowd gasps, a constable pushes through the mass of people to take charge, a woman sobs – but nobody considers that they would be safer indoors. So it was for Susan and me. As we went about our unlawful business, I saw a pickpocket taken up by a constable and, for a moment, I reflected that we might share his fate, but then we saw a card case in a shop window and moved mechanically into our, by now well-rehearsed, routine.

We took our lunch at the Pantheon, walking through the imposing columns of the Oxford Street entrance like a couple of swells. We had yet to work our business in this place. It called itself a bazaar rather than a department store and, despite its elaborate architecture, I had not realised what a great variety of goods were sold there. Its appearance suggested that it had once been very grand, but it was clearly past its best. Many of the shops catered for children and Susan was captivated by the monkeys gambolling in a pet shop window. While she was thus occupied I looked about and noticed that the variety of businesses operating under this roof provided an ideal opportunity for us to pass off a considerable amount of coin in one afternoon.

Susan's excitement as the monkeys bounded over to grimace at her through the glass drew me back to the present. I wished I could share her simple delight in small things. For myself, I was appalled at how quickly and completely I had taken to the criminal life, so that where others saw innocent amusement, I saw only the opportunity for deception.

At least I could pause from my felonious labour and enjoy our meal. We made our way to the tea rooms, where a light luncheon (cold ham and tongue with salad) was served while we watched the fish swimming around the fountain that decorated the centre of the place. Despite the background bustle of women – for they were mainly women – coming and going, it was peaceful and, for the first time in a while, I felt I could relax. The lettuce was wilting and the pieces of celery in the salad far from crisp, but my companion pronounced it excellent. She was, under it all, a nice girl, and I imagine that, if life had been kinder to her, she might have worked in a shop or, perhaps, even been a governess. As it was, her outings with me were a pleasant break from the usual way she earned her bread. I could see no obvious signs of pox, but if she were not infected now, I was sure she would be soon.

'Let's order arrowroot cake.' She sounded like a little girl being treated for her birthday. 'They say that's special here.'

I had not the heart to deny her. We both ate the arrowroot cake. It was lighter than most cakes – an advantage of the arrowroot, I supposed – but there was a trace of bitterness to it that the sugar liberally sprinkled on top failed to disguise. I must admit that I was unimpressed, but Susan was thrilled. 'Well,' she said, 'I've eaten at the Pantheon and had their famous cake. Won't the other girls be jealous?'

We paid with real money. I told myself it was because the waiter would have too much time to check the coins as he went to get our change, but, in truth, I think it was because I wanted that little interlude of innocence to last as long as I could make it.

From Oxford Street, though, we bent our way to Seven Dials. How wide the chasm that separated the two, though we walked less than a mile between them! There I gave Michael the proceeds of our morning's endeavours and bade Susan farewell for the time being. I went to my lodgings and changed from the clothes which I had used in my 'respectable' guise to those which would be more suited to an evening of drinking in the public houses frequented by printers.

That night I had resolved to try a house called, appropriately enough, The Printer's Arms. Printers generally pleasant enough company and happy to talk for the price of a pint. As the afternoon wore on, men would arrive at the end of their day's work, while in early evening they would be joined by those employed in the newspaper trade, preparing themselves to face a night's toil.

I had arrived early, because I was looking amongst those who had worked on their own account, rather than being employed by a newspaper. I passed a pleasant enough couple of hours and learned more than I really cared to about the vagaries of the printer's trade, but I heard no news of any printers with engraving skills whose condition might encourage them to join our enterprise. As the evening wore on and the place became more crowded with newspaper men loudly demanding their drinks be hurried to them before the shift started, I thought I should be getting home. Then I imagined myself sleepless in my lonely bed, and decided to take another pint.

It was good that I did. On the table next to me a group of men – from the *Morning Herald*, as far as I could judge – were complaining about a new foreman. 'He had no business to sack Jack Underhill,' one was saying, loud in his annoyance.

I listened, as much from force of habit, as from any idea that a newspaper typesetter would be any use to me.

Another man joined in the complaint. 'The block would not be used again. What matter if Underhill had scratched a few changes on it?'

It was not the loss of the block that had led to Underhill's dismissal apparently, but that the changes were considered obscene.

'I'd have thought that giving him a prick improved his appearance no end.'

There was laughter, but then the first man slapped his hand on the table. 'I don't see it's a laughing matter when a decent man is on the streets and him with a wife and three kids. He'll get no reference from the *Herald*.'

The laughter died abruptly and the men supped silently for a moment. It was my opportunity.

'Gentleman, do I understand that Mr Underhill is an engraver?'

The man who had condemned the laughter looked up at me suspiciously. 'Who wants to know?'

'My name is Mr Turner.' It seemed wiser not to give my own name and the artist's had come first to mind, on account of the subject being engraving. 'I am looking for a man who can assist me with some engravings of ...' I hesitated and then concluded, 'a delicate nature.'

It seemed best. Given the snatch of conversation I had heard, it seemed likely that Mr Underhill would be adept at producing the obscene pictures which were so popular with a certain class of reader. Better that his friends think that this was the nature of my commission than that I allowed a glimpse of the truth.

The man grinned at me. 'I'm Frank,' he said and gave me an ink-stained hand to shake. 'Yes, Jack Underhill might well be your man if you have *delicate*' (he made the word sound utterly disgusting) 'work you want doing.'

I bought him a drink. It seemed expected. Then I bought all his friends a drink. That seemed expected too. Only then did we turn to the matter of how I might find Jack Underhill.

I think they were genuinely concerned for their friend, or they could have been slower to give me the information I wanted and demanded a higher price for it. As it was, for the few pennies I spent on beer I got the address of the man I hoped would be able to help me.

'You'll have to be quick, mind. He won't be able to make the rent next week, an' him and his family will be on the street.'

I thanked them, bought another round of drinks and left. They were right. I had no time to lose, but it was full dark by now and scarcely the time to call at the poor man's house. Besides, Michael would need to approve my choice and agree on what conditions he was to join us.

I hurried towards Marylebone and my lodgings. The gas lamps cast pools of light that seemed to intensify the shadows between them rather than increase the overall illumination of the streets. The gloom suited my mood. I had solved one problem but it seemed to be drawing me further into the web of conspiracy in which I had become entangled.

I thought of my nameless tormentor from the Home Office. How would he respond to my news? I could already imagine him sneering: 'But you have yet to meet the bad baronet, haven't you?' I swerved aside to avoid the beggar sat near one of the lamps.

I peered cautiously into the gloom. The police generally moved beggars on here. Was he simply a poor indigent or were there friends of his, waiting in the dark to rob me?

The only sound was my own footsteps and the heavy breathing of the man under the lamp, wrapped in a bundle of rags. He was, I decided, no threat, and I set course for the next street lamp. My thoughts returned to Sir Charles Crawley. Perhaps, now that I had found a possible engraver, it was time to insist that I meet the mysterious head of our enterprise.

Yes, before I was ensnared still further, I would demand to meet Sir Charles.

I arrived in Queen Street next morning prepared for a fight with Michael. He had shown no sign of introducing me to Sir Charles and I did not expect him to agree that I should see him now. When I suggested a meeting, though, he acquiesced almost straightaway.

'If you think we might be able to engrave our own plates, you definitely need to talk to Charlie about it. I'm surprised you haven't asked to see him before.'

I was reminded of the city in the psalm. *Wickedness is in the midst thereof: deceit and guile depart not from her streets.* So much had deceit and guile become a part of my life in this city that the possibility that I might innocently have asked for what I wanted had never occurred to me.

What did this say about the person I was becoming?

I returned Michael's smile, but I felt that my face was a mask, and that where he offered honest friendship, I was, indeed, harbouring naught but deceit and guile.

I changed no false coins that day but went straight to the address I had been given for Underhill. It was a respectable little house in one of the long rows of workers' terraces being built for the navvies just South of the Thames. I knocked at the door which was opened cautiously. I guessed that they were already nervous of the landlord's representatives.

The woman who eventually admitted me had eyes red from crying, but her husband, when summoned to the front passage of that little house, looked more enraged than distressed. Was I from the paper? Was I from the landlord? Was there any good reason he should not beat me and tell me to go to hell? The fury bubbled from him in a series of questions that I think he had no particular desire to hear me answer. It was enough for him that he was angry and that he could vent his anger on me.

Eventually the torrent of questions and abuse paused long enough for me to insist that I was a friend and might be in a position to offer him work. Could I, perhaps, take him for a drink?

The idea that I might buy him a pint completely changed the way in which he viewed me and, in the time that it took him to put on a jacket and a respectable hat, he was out of the house and leading me to the Railway Arms. 'It will be quiet there at this time of day,' he said, 'the navvies all being out working on the track.'

The Railway Arms seemed a respectable enough place, although it was doubtless livelier in the evenings. The public bar was large but, as my new friend had promised, it was almost empty. I bought two pints at the bar and carried them to a table in the corner, remote from any listening ears.

'I understand you are an engraver.'

'I engrave from drawings made up for the newspapers,' he admitted. 'I am no artist.'

'But you can copy from a drawing?'

'Of course I can.' His tone suggested that he was insulted at the very idea of his abilities being questioned.

'Exactly?'

'I've said I can, haven't I?' The rage was beginning to bubble up again.

I had brought with me a piece of patterned lace, purchased especially for this interview. I withdrew it from my pocket and placed it on the table in front of him. 'What about that? Could you copy that pattern precisely?'

Underhill snatched the lace from my hand and began to examine it. The anger faded from his face as he became totally absorbed in looking at the pattern before him.

'Yes,' he said at last. 'I can copy that.'

'How much would you charge?'

He gave me a shrewd look. 'You don't want someone to engrave pictures of lace for you.'

'No.' There was no point in lying. 'This is an exercise, to see if you're as good as they say you are.'

He looked at it again. 'When people come looking for a printer to do some engraving, private like, it's usually dirty pictures they're after. You don't want dirty pictures, do you?'

'No,' I said. 'I don't.'

He made great play of taking another swig from his beer. 'If you're after what I think you're after, it's Botany Bay if we're caught.'

'Can you do it?'

We were no longer talking about the lace, and we both knew it. There was a very long silence.

'I've a wife and family.'

'You just do the engraving. I'm the only one who will know who you are.' This was almost certain to be a lie, but if my wishing it might make it so, then it should be the truth. In any case, it needed to be said. 'I'll make sure your name is kept out of it.'

Still nothing.

'I can give you the week's rent while you think about it.'

His face twisted into a bitter simulacrum of a smile. 'You know I have no choice, don't you?'

'No job. No references. You have a choice and I'm offering you a week to think about it. You can do the work we want, or you can starve.' Some might think I was being cruel, but the situation was not of my making. I was presenting him with the simple truth, and he was man enough to accept it.

'I'll do the work.'

'What will you need?'

He picked the lace up and fiddled with it. 'I'll need the lace, of course. The exact pattern that you want.' I nodded. 'And an engraving block. I have my own tools, but I'll need the block.'

I nodded again. It made sense that he would want us to provide the blank block on which he would make the engraving. Blocks cost money and he had none. It was not surprising that he had his own tools. Indeed, I would have had my doubts about his quality if he had not, for a good artisan would make sure that he always had the tools of his trade to hand.

'Acid?'

No, he said, he would not want acid. 'Perhaps a little, but I have that. This is going to be very fine work. I'll cut most of the block by hand, a scratch at a time.'

I pushed some money across the table to him. 'Rent,' I said. 'I need to speak to my principal and then I'll be in touch. This should keep you going until then.'

His hand fell on the coins and he slid them across the table, vanishing them into a pocket. Then he gave me a brisk nod, rose to his feet and left.

I sat and finished my beer and thought about the conversation we had just had. For all I knew, this was the first criminal act Underhill had ever been involved in. How easily circumstances can make villains of us all.

I thought of my own circumstances and suddenly the beer tasted sour in my mouth. I put down my glass and started back towards home.

I wore my 'respectable' clothes that evening. Sir Charles, it seemed to me, owed much of his mastery of Seven Dials to the natural respect which the working classes offer to the aristocracy regardless of the personal qualities of the individual. I decided that I would dress as a gentleman, in order that we might meet on more equal terms than when he was lording it over the poor. In any case, Michael had told me that we were to dine at Sir Charles' residence on the edge of Soho. It was not an especially prosperous area – indeed it was reputed that many of the houses there were places of assignation. All the same, the address was at least notionally respectable, and I judged that the clothes I had selected would be appropriate.

We were to dine early. I had arranged to meet Michael at Regent's Circus, as I had no desire to venture into Seven Dials of an evening while wearing clothes that proclaimed me an outsider. I waited for him near the Black Horse Inn. There was usually a crowd of idlers around the entertainment room there and it seemed a natural place to meet. I stood quietly, watching folk come and go until, shortly before eight o'clock, Michael appeared.

I hurried to greet him. 'I was worried that I might have missed you, with so many people about.'

He led me quickly towards Golden Square, but we turned off before we reached it. Our destination turned out to be, ironically, on Queen Street – but a very different sort of Queen Street from the one where Michael lived. The houses, though by no means impressive, were decent and well kept up. Where Queen Street in Seven Dials had broken windows and doors askew in their frames, this Queen Street offered a parade of sparkling glass and door knockers that shone golden where they caught the rays of the evening sun.

Michael lifted the knocker at number fifteen. I imagined the sound echoing, like something out of a novel by Edgar Allan Poe, but I'm sure that was just my imagination. The door, when it opened, did not creak ominously; no ravens were perched in the hall. Instead, a nondescript man in an inexpensive suit extended his hand in greeting.

'Good evening. You must be Mr Williamson. I'm so pleased to meet you.' Then, apparently perceiving the confusion on my face, he explained, 'We don't stand on ceremony here. The days when I could afford a butler are long gone. I answer my own door now.'

So this was Sir Charles Crawley. He was not at all what I had expected. Michael's account suggested a man with a marked physical presence, while the Home Office apparently had me pursuing some evil mastermind of espionage who, I suppose, might look like anything – but surely not like this. He was a little shorter than me, with mousy hair, thinning on top. He had the sort of small, fussy face that looks as if it should have been completed with a pince-nez, but he wore no eyeglasses of any kind. I would have thought him a minor clerk, or possibly a small shopkeeper. Still, I returned his handshake, which was rather firmer than I had expected from his looks, and he led the way into the house.

'There are just the three of us, so this is by nature of an informal gathering. I thought that, in the circumstances, we might go straight into dinner.'

Michael and I made murmurs of agreement as Sir Charles opened the door to his right and gestured for us to enter.

The hallway had been barely furnished and the decor showed signs of neglect, so I was unprepared for the sight of what appeared a large mahogany dining table, neatly covered with a cloth of white damask. Half-a-dozen chairs were tucked under each of the long sides of the table, but just three places had been set at one end. Such an arrangement meant, of course, that the careful symmetry of a formal table setting was impossible. Even so, a fine silver tureen of soup had been placed in front of the host's seat, while side dishes stood ready, conveniently to hand for the guests to pass.

'My apologies for having the table prepared already. There's only one girl to serve, so she sets it before my guests arrive. Still, the soup is steaming, which is always a good sign.'

I was placed to Sir Charles' right and Michael sat at his left and he wasted no time ladling soup for both of us. It was an oxtail, and very good. Sir Charles might have only one girl to serve, but I warranted he had a fine cook. More impressive, even, than the soup, were the bowls into which it was served. My time in India had given me an appreciation of fine china, as the English community there vied with each other to ship out more and more impressive dinner services. My soup was being served onto Coalport china. If I had any doubt (and I could hardly lift the plate to check the maker's mark) the delicate flowers that decorated the centrepiece confirmed it. Sir Charles may no longer have been rich, but he had clearly had money in the past.

The soup was finished and the girl entered to clear it. She was dressed smartly enough, her apron crisp and white, but there was a look about her face that I recognised from Seven Dials – the expression of one for whom life holds no promise but the promise of degradation. I noticed that Sir Charles' eyes followed her movements with an almost predatory intensity, while hers were kept downcast, avoiding meeting the gaze of any of us. She had been trained well enough, though, and the soup tureen was duly replaced with a roast, which our host enthusiastically carved, slicing generous portions. Both the sight and the smell promised that cook and butcher had conspired to produce the best that English beef can offer, and I was not disappointed.

Although our host had promised us an informal meal, the quality of the food seemed to discourage anything but the normal social niceties in the way of conversation. I learned that Sir Charles' family had lived in this area for generations. 'Alas, I am the last of that distinguished line, reduced to haunting this old house like my own ghost.'

I probed, as much as conventional politeness would allow, for the reasons for the collapse of his family fortunes. They were not long in disclosing themselves.

'My mother was a beautiful woman, but sickly. She never really recovered from my birth. The idea of a larger family was impossible, so I was always doomed to be an only child. She died when I was ten.'

I made appropriately sympathetic noises. 'And your father?'

Sir Charles' face darkened. 'He died five years ago.'

'My sympathies, sir. It is a hard thing to lose a parent.'

'Harder when the parent dies by his own hand.'

There was an uncomfortable silence broken only by the clinking of cutlery on bone china.

Michael was the first to speak. 'It's good news that John has found us a printer, is it not?'

With a visible effort, Sir Charles brought his mind back from whatever dark places it had been exploring. He did not, however, give his attention to Michael. Instead, he turned to me.

'You did a good job, there, Mr Williamson. I had no idea that it might be possible to find the man we need so easily.'

'You are happy that I recruit him to join us?'

Sir Charles took another mouthful of beef and chewed carefully while he seemed to consider this reply.

'I don't think he will be joining us, exactly. At least, not just yet. I think we should look on him more as an independent supplier. I understand he does not know your name.'

'I am Mr Turner to the gentleman.'

Sir Charles permitted himself a smile. 'Very droll,' he said. He dabbed his lips carefully with his napkin. 'If, by any mischance, this man should come to the notice of the authorities, I can see no way in which he could be linked to us.'

I shook my head.

'In that case, what have we to lose?' Only at this point, did Sir Charles deign to look towards Michael, who responded with a barely perceptible shake of his head.

'Well then, we're agreed.' He placed his knife and fork carefully on his plate. 'We get the engraving done and then we're in business.'

I saw Michael open his mouth to object and hurried to speak before he could say anything. Sir Charles was going to take this better coming from me.

'I fear it's not as simple as that, sir.'

Sir Charles turned to face me. He was obviously trying to keep his expression neutral, but a little twitch on his top lip betrayed his irritation.

'We need the paper.'

Sir Charles turned to Michael, who nodded his agreement. 'The Bank of England uses a very high-quality paper with a watermark. That's going to be the problem.'

The lip was twitching more violently now. 'You must have been aware of this all along. Why press ahead if we weren't going to be able to finish the job?'

Now was the moment to find out if Sir Charles had

secret backers – the French government or anybody else. I leaned forward. 'You must know people, sir.' I hoped that flattery might lull him into betraying himself. 'If any of us can get a supply of the paper, I'm sure you can.'

'Don't be a bloody fool.' He snapped at me and then, as if recollecting his manners, he forced a smile. 'I'm sorry, Mr Williamson. You mean well, of course, but I just don't have those connections. If I did, I doubt that I would be running a forgery operation from a cellar in Queen Street.'

It seemed to me that it was not him that was running the operation, but Michael. More importantly, he spoke of it as his own operation and he had no hidden backer who could help with the paper. Surely this was evidence that even the Home Office could not ignore. There was no French plot. There never had been. Once my anonymous nemesis had called on me again and I had told him what I now knew, I could extricate myself from this whole situation. Michael, too, would be safe – safe enough, at any rate, to slip quietly away from Queen Street. Meanwhile, though, I needed to calm my host. His anger could not damage me, but I had Michael to think of.

'If we can buy some paper of about the same quality, we can press a mark into it with wire. It will pass as a watermark provided it is not examined too closely.'

Michael leaned forward, similarly reassuring. 'We'll make sure the notes are carried around a bit and get crumpled and dirty. It makes them more trustworthy if they look like they've been used and it makes it harder to spot any little mistakes.'

Sir Charles leaned back in his seat. The twitching in his lip grew less marked as I watched. He did not speak, but seemed to be considering what we had said. Then he smiled, as if satisfied, and turned his attention back to the food. 'Dessert, gentlemen?'

Relieved to have moved back onto safer ground, we both nodded.

'Where is that wretched girl?' Sir Charles reached to a glass bell conveniently to hand beside his place setting. It made a sharp tinkling sound that brought the servant hurrying back into the room.

'Dessert, Mary. You should not need to be told.'

'No, sir. I'm sorry, sir.' The girl mumbled her apologies as she gathered plates up in what looked like a panic.

In India, of course, a score of servants would help. I knew that no English household could afford so many, but the task was obviously beyond one poor girl. Her desperate efforts seemed to me to be so ridiculous that they were almost humorous, but then I saw the look on Michael's face. He did not think it funny at all. It was only then that I realised the hold that Sir Charles had over those he controlled. Mouse-like and inoffensive as he had appeared to me, it seemed that the men and women who served him lived in fear of his anger.

I looked back at Sir Charles. The lip was twitching, albeit slowly, and there was a look in his eyes that did not bode well for Mary.

We waited in silence for the few minutes it took the girl to remove the evidence of our meal. As she left the room, though, Sir Charles remarked, in a voice that she could hardly fail to have heard, that she had been hired from the lists produced by 'The Female Aid Society'.

'It exists, so it says, to save women desirous of leaving a life of depravity. I thought it my Christian duty to turn to them for domestic assistance, but I fear I may have been foolish. The girl is clearly not up to the job.'

A few minutes later she returned with the dessert. Little had changed in her expression, which seemed to be naturally formed for misery, but her eyes were red and I think she had allowed herself a few tears while she was out of the room.

She had brought in a cabinet pudding which was, like

the rest of the meal, excellent. The mood, though, had been broken and I could not relax and enjoy it.

As soon as we put down our spoons, Mary hurried in to remove our plates and place a port decanter on our host's right. He poured himself a generous glass and passed the bottle to me. 'Can't be passing it to the left with just the three of us,' he said.

After Michael had had the chance to fill his glass, Sir Charles raised a toast. 'The Queen, God bless her.' I looked for any trace of satirical intent, but I saw none and joined him willingly. Only in Michael's almost imperceptible hesitation did I see any indication that he might appreciate the irony of toasting the monarch whose currency we debased for our livelihood.

It had been a peculiar, and not entirely comfortable, evening, and nobody seemed in a mood to extend it. Once the port was drunk, we soon rose to go. Sir Charles led us to the front door to bid us farewell but, as I passed, he laid a hand upon my arm.

'It was good to meet you, Mr Williamson. Perhaps we can take lunch together soon.'

I wanted to recoil, but I controlled my emotion. It could do me no harm to know more about the man and his plans. He may not be an agent of the French, but he was, I judged, an evil man. If I could learn anything that would help end his career, it was best that I should. So it was that I smiled and nodded politely and he promised that he would send me a note at my lodgings.

Michael had waited on the pavement and we set off together, though our paths would part at the end of the street.

'He's a fine man, isn't he?' said Michael.

I was astonished. 'He's a brute,' I said.

Michael stopped and turned to me, looking at me much as he had when we had first met and he judged me a gentleman from the cut of my cloth.

119

'You still don't understand, do you, John?' He was not angry, but sounded suddenly tired. 'Charlie took me up when I was lost. I would have died, and he saved me.'

'He's a bully and a thug. He set his men on your Harry.'

'Yes. Yes, he did. But life for those of us who live in Seven Dials is hard, John. You have to be hard to survive. Or have a friend who can protect you, as Harry has me.'

'And your Charlie protects you?'

'Charlie gave me a chance. Nobody else did.'

He started again to the end of the street and I followed him. At the corner, I bade him farewell. 'I'm off home. I imagine you are too.'

'Not straight away,' he said. 'Got to see a man about a dog.'

'Ah, yes. Harry said something about meetings.' And so had my mysterious friend from the Home Office. 'More education?'

'No.' Michael could not have looked more shifty if he had tried. 'Well … yes, in a manner of speaking.'

'So where do you go?'

He mumbled something about 'just seeing a few mates'.

Until now, I had not thought much about my visitor's interest in how Michael spent his evenings but his whole manner now so strongly suggested some sort of conspiracy that I began to wonder if I had been right to be so dismissive of it.

'Well, if it's a secret –' I said.

I had obviously taken the right approach. Michael was embarrassed by the suggestion that he was keeping something from me.

'Look, there's just a few mates, but I'll ask, and maybe we can all invite you to the next meeting.'

I shrugged in genuine perplexity.

'I'll explain tomorrow,' said Michael, and he was gone.

CHAPTER SEVEN

Back at my lodgings, I hurried up the stairs to my room, confident that I would find that I had a visitor. I was not to be disappointed.

'So you've finally met Sir Charles,' he greeted me, in his usual arrogant drawl.

After our last exchange, I was determined to at least maintain some sort of dignity.

'You might give me time to take off my hat.'

I removed my hat, ostentatiously turning my back on my visitor as I restored it safely to its place on top of my wardrobe. 'I'm surprised you need me as your spy. You already seem to know everything that's going on.'

'We know all the comings and goings. We don't know what goes on inside. For example, what did you and Sir Charles have to discuss?'

'Ah, yes.' I allowed myself a smile, settled myself on the bed – my visitor had again taken the only chair – and delivered the information that I hoped would put a stop to this whole charade.

'We discussed the fact that not only can Sir Charles not obtain printing blocks for currency notes, but he has no access to the paper either. I asked him if he had friends who might help with this and he insisted that he had not. As I recall …' I closed my eyes and tilted my head back, recollecting the scene, 'his exact words were that he had "no connections that could assist him". I think, sir, that this information should put an end to the suggestion that this is a French plot.'

'Hmm.' Now it was my visitor's turn to close his eyes

as he considered what I had said. When he opened them, though, they were alive with the energy I associate with a tiger that has just caught site of a tethered goat.

'I don't think we can write off the French just like that. They can be cunning, these Frogs. No, if Napoleon has a hand in this, it will not be obvious. In this case the beggars' (I hope he said 'beggars') 'may be being particularly crafty. Have you discovered how your Michael Radford spends his evenings yet?'

I shook my head. Suddenly I was no longer confident that my involvement with the Home Office was going to be over with the end of this meeting.

'Mr Radford …' He steepled his fingers with the same smug assurance as on his last visit. 'Mr Radford has been drinking in Great Windmill Street.'

I stared at him in genuine perplexity.

'At the German Workers' Educational Society.'

'But Mr Radford isn't German.'

For once, the man from the Home Office allowed his mask of urbanity to slip and his irritation to show.

'Don't be so obtuse. The Society isn't for Germans, its members are only incidentally workers and they educate themselves in little but revolution.'

My face must have revealed that this outburst had left me no wiser.

'They're Communists, man! Great Windmill Street is where the wretched Herr Marx spreads his insidious propaganda. Hence "German", you see.'

I didn't, exactly, but I supposed things were becoming slightly clearer. 'But the Communists are against kings, aren't they?' My visitor said nothing, so I plunged on. 'They're hardly likely to be plotting with Napoleon.'

He shook his head, almost sorrowfully, as a teacher might shake his at a particularly dull-witted pupil.

'They're revolutionaries, Williamson. They want to strike England down. They will use any tool to that end.'

'And the French?'

He nodded, again with that sorrowful expression. 'The perfidy of the French knows no bounds. They will cabal with anybody. This Herr Marx is wanted by the German state. The French will be more than happy to plot together with a person the Germans view as an enemy.'

He made it sound so convincing that for a moment I wondered if it might be true. Could Michael indeed be a Communist, plotting with the King of France to strike down England by destroying its currency?

I looked at the man from the Home Office and saw him suddenly for what he was – an anonymous bureaucrat in a mindless machine. I thought of Michael: his love for Harry; his awe of Sir Charles; his touching faith that his studies at the Mechanics Institute could enable him to improve his station in life. Was I seriously expected to believe that he was a Communist, infected with some radical German dogma that would turn him against his own country? Was he supposed to be plotting simultaneously with French Royalists and German Republicans?

It was ludicrous. But if the Home Office could give serious consideration to such rubbish, they were clearly not amenable to either reason or evidence. I rose and, bowing to my visitor, told him that his news had filled me with horror and that I would do everything in my power to stop the plot. Then, as quickly as I decently could, I ushered him out of my room.

Once he had gone, I sat and tried to compose my thoughts.

The first thing, it seemed to me, was to establish where Michael had been that evening.

The next day, as soon as I arrived at Queen Street, I reminded him of his promise to see if I could join him at one of his meetings.

We were, as usual when we had business to discuss, sat

in his room, Harry buzzing about with tea and biscuits. He would have insisted on making me breakfast, too, but I explained that this meal was included in the price of my lodgings.

'I know the sort of meal a landlady will give you,' Harry insisted. 'You'll be needing more than that to see you through the day. Let me give you some bread and butter.'

'John's fine, Harry.' Michael smiled indulgently, like a mother happy to see her child showing off its skills.

'Well, have another biscuit anyway.'

I took a biscuit while Michael told me how he'd spent the evening. 'I was at choir practice, John.'

I allowed myself to look sceptical. 'So why all the secrecy?'

'It's a club for working men. There's singing, drawing, even dancing classes. And there's some practical stuff – I'm learning a little German.'

'Is it a German club?' I asked, perhaps a little too quickly.

'It started as a German club, as a matter of fact. But it's got all sorts in now.' He looked puzzled for a moment. 'Why did you ask? Have you heard of it?'

'It was just that you said you were learning German.'

I thought my answer unconvincing, but it seemed to satisfy him. 'The truth is, though,' he continued, 'that they're political as well. It means they don't really want strangers coming to meetings.'

'Political?'

He smiled and shrugged. 'They supported the Chartists a couple of years ago.'

'Chartists, then.'

Harry had come back into the room with another pot of tea, which he slammed onto the table with uncharacteristic force. 'They're not Chartists. Go on, Michael, tell him who you've got mixed up with.'

It was the first time I had ever heard Harry speak sharply to his lover and Michael squirmed like any henpecked husband. 'Well, truth to tell,' he mumbled, eyeing Harry nervously, 'they call themselves Communists.'

I had never imagined that you could demonstrate anger by the simple process of pouring tea into a cup, but Harry did it. 'They're nothing but trouble, Michael. You should leave them alone.'

'They do talk about politics,' Michael admitted, turning to me. 'But it's all interesting stuff, about capital and labour and the role of the bourgeoisie. Sometimes someone will talk about revolutions in Europe, but they mean no harm here.'

Harry was muttering to himself as he cleared the table. There were to be no more biscuits this morning. 'No harm! German revolutionaries plotting in London and they mean no harm.'

Michael tried to laugh off Harry's anger, turning to me for support. But I could not offer him any. I knew little about Communism, but I knew that revolutionaries were scheming and bombing across the whole of Europe. Our own country had been spared these ravages because of the wisdom of our rulers and the loyalty of our people. I understood, though, why the Home Office considered them a threat and kept them under observation.

'Are you a Communist?'

'No! I mean, you have to pledge an oath and …'

'But you go to their meetings?'

'I go to the singing and – well, some of the other stuff.'

Harry had been standing listening, with his arms folded across his chest. 'You go on Mondays.'

Michael said nothing, but the guilt on his face meant I had to ask. 'What happens on Mondays?'

Harry interrupted before he could answer. 'Mondays and Tuesdays they talk politics. Michael loves it. He comes home and he's full of proletariat this and crisis of that. They have people come special to talk to them. Michael went to a lecture once on a Sunday. He made me go with him. There was some German fellow who said that the working people would rise up and destroy the country. It was disgusting.'

Michael tried a tired smile. 'I think you took it too literally, Harry. Mr Engels is one of their leaders and his father owns a factory in Manchester. I doubt he's going to lead a revolution that will burn down the family firm.'

I opened my mouth to argue, but then thought better of it. Instead, I asked, 'Do these people know anything about the coining?'

'Of course not.' Michael's outrage was clearly genuine. 'What kind of an idiot do you think I am?'

I did not answer. I thought he was the kind of idiot who would go to Communist meetings and who might even have Communist sympathies. He did not, however, seem to me a person who would plot with Communists to devalue his country's currency. His motivations were criminal rather than political. It was doubtful, though, that the Home Office would agree with me.

Our discussion left the dangerous subject of Michael's friends in Great Windmill Street and moved on to the business of printing the bank notes.

My first task was to obtain a clean five-pound note that could be used as a model by our engraver. This turned out to be less straightforward than I had imagined. My initial notion was simply to go to my bank and withdraw the money but the note that I was given had been folded and one corner was grubby. Mr Underhill, I was sure, would want to prick out the pattern and an unfolded, unblemished note would make the task much easier. One takes a five-pound note for granted these days, but in truth they do not often make an appearance in everyday transactions. I asked Michael if he had a five-pound note and he laughed, suggesting that if his life featured five-pound notes he would hardly be staying in Queen Street.

At least the grubby note gave me an indication of the sort of paper that I would need. Michael, who had clearly looked into the matter, told me that the paper of forged notes is usually of a darker colour, so I was to look out for paper of the highest quality. With my five pounds safe in my pocket as a guide, I visited several stationers looking for the best quality paper that they could provide. None, of course, had exactly the texture of the currency note, but I eventually tracked down a linen-based paper that was similar in weight, a brilliant white, and did not tear easily. I bought a sheet, and Michael and I cut pieces the size of the notes and carried them in our pockets for a couple of days to see what they looked like after use. The result was gratifying: once the paper had been handled, the difference in the exact shade was not obvious. Although a new currency note has a distinct feel, the product of its weight and the quality of its manufacture, my old note was already losing its distinctive texture as I folded and unfolded it each time I compared it with other papers. By now, it felt less like most people imagined a note should feel than did the paper we were experimenting with.

We had to be careful, though. Five pounds is a great deal of money and not something that is handled too casually. If we allowed our paper to become too dirty, it would make people wary of it. In any case, being of inferior quality to the Bank's paper, too much use would render it limp and unconvincing. The secret, then, was to judge the amount of wear that would disguise the note's failures as genuine currency, but which would not itself produce suspicion.

Simple as this exercise appeared, it occupied a significant amount of time and attention over the next few days.

This was not, of course, the only thing that we were

doing. There was the regular business of coining to attend to. I have described the place as appearing like a factory and, as with any factory, there was always work for the managers to do. I still took false sovereigns out from time to time but we did not want my face to become known, so I more often supervised. Men had to be despatched with the tin and rewarded when they had disposed of it. We used the men who lived in Queen Street to change the silver in public houses, but I recruited men of more respectable appearance to change the sovereigns. As I had noticed on my first visit to Seven Dials, there were always some men – burglars usually – who had recently pulled off a successful job and they would often dress themselves in finery with their proceeds. These could be used occasionally, though their faces were often too well known to be trusted within a mile or more, so I supplemented them with others who were new to a life of crime. My time spent learning about printers who had fallen on hard times came in useful here. These were decent men whose desperation, now that they had lost their livelihood, made them amenable to the suggestion that they might turn a blind eye to the law. Once kitted out in a smart suit, they could easily convince people that they were successful small businessmen and they handed over sovereigns quite naturally. I discovered that many of their erstwhile colleagues, who still made a precarious living from their craft, were not averse to buying supplies of ink and paper without enquiring too closely as to their provenance. I therefore sent some of my recruits to their old suppliers where, claiming to be back in business, they purchased materials which we sold on to their struggling former competitors. We even bought our own printing press with a mix of real and false coins, collecting it in a stolen cart, which vanished (together with our printer accomplice) before the fraud was detected.

Michael was much taken with this exploit, which he

considered criminal legerdemain of the highest order, and he boasted of it to Sir Charles, who was reminded to ask me to luncheon with him, as he had promised more than a week before.

Lunch was a more pleasant affair than dinner. An informal lunch is a natural thing, while the mixture of easy manners and formal silverware that had marked our dinner had been uncomfortable. To my relief, Sir Charles told me as soon as I arrived that the girl, Mary, was not in attendance.

'I had to give that dreadful girl her notice and I have yet to replace her. But never mind, we'll have a jolly bachelor lunch.'

Mary might have gone, but I warranted the same cook was somewhere on the premises, for lunch was excellent. Some was clearly left over from the night before: a cold chicken missing one leg and cold veal pie with a slice already taken, but the ham and the tongue appeared untouched and had presumably been bought specifically for this meal. There was bread and cheese and both wine and ale had been laid out.

Sir Charles gestured to a seat. 'Make yourself at home.'

I sat and, taking him at his word, poured myself some wine. He smiled his approval. 'Michael would have taken the beer.'

I took a sip from my glass, feeling that I had somehow let my friend down with my choice of beverage. 'I do not think less of a man because he prefers beer.'

'It tells you, though, what sort of a man he is.'

'An honest man, brought up in the countryside.'

My host raised his eyebrows at my use of the word 'honest'. I could have cheerfully bitten my tongue off, but, far from making fun of my slip, Sir Charles responded sympathetically. 'The priests talk of the sin of Adam, but I sometimes think that we are all born honest. It is circumstance that turns us into villains.'

I felt I was seeing a different side to Sir Charles with the two of us alone together. Perhaps he thought that with me, a stranger and a gentleman, he could reveal himself in a way that he could not when he was with Michael. I said nothing, really. I just made the appropriate noises of encouragement from time to time and listened. All men like to talk about themselves and he was no exception.

Charlie, as he insisted I call him, was proud of his title. At the same time, though, he resented the fact that, as a baronet, he was considered the very lowest form of aristocrat. 'Every ermine-clad clown considers himself better than me,' he complained. He was utterly unaware of the irony of his views, given the air of superiority he unthinkingly adopted when dealing with the men and women of Seven Dials. 'The title has been in my family for generations. I deserve some respect. Damn it! The title deserves some respect.'

It seemed that his family had been trying to live up to their title since before the time of King George II. Despite their pretensions, money had slipped slowly but surely away.

'Then the pater had the idea of buying railway shares. He bought early, before they were popular, and suddenly we had all the money we had always deserved. We bought this place. There was a proper staff. I was going to make the Tour; I'd been having extra French lessons because I thought they'd help. Then the railway company crashed.'

He drained his wine glass at this point in the tale, filled it, and drained it again.

'That's when the pater killed himself.' Loathsome as I found Sir Charles Crawley, it was difficult not to feel some sympathy for him. He was barely into his twenties and suddenly the man of the house. He'd been shocked by his father's death, but a meeting with his banker soon revealed why the man had committed suicide.

'We were horribly in debt. The servants were all owed

money, which was not so bad, because they had board here and weren't likely to chuck their places up in a hurry. But the tradesmen were owed money too, and it's difficult to keep the house and staff once the butcher won't deliver and the greengrocer insists on ready money before he will hand over so much as a potato.'

His father had realised too late that he was over invested in railway shares and had tried to diversify by buying houses in Battersea and renting them out to the railway company to house their navvies.

'Of course, when the railways were in trouble, they didn't need the houses anymore. They'd been bought with borrowed money and now we couldn't raise a decent rent on them.'

The houses in Battersea went, but it left Sir Charles with an idea. 'Rent's more reliable than dividends. The railway company stopped paying us, but London is growing all the time. It's full of people looking for somewhere to live. My problem was that after the debts were cleared there was nothing to buy new houses with.'

The answer, he decided, was to forget about buying decent rows of new terraced housing and find something cheap that he could fill with London's growing army of the poor and homeless.

'In the end, I did even better. I found Seven Dials. Houses there aren't cheap – they're free.' All you needed, he realised, was a few large men with sticks to clear the squatters out of a property, which you could then claim for yourself.

'Well, I had enough money for that. There are plenty of men who'll break a leg for you if you give them a florin.' Better yet, he soon realised that he could offer accommodation rent-free to men who would help enforce his control over the other tenants. 'It is the best of businesses. As you take over more houses, you generate not only more rent, but more bodies are available to you to extend your enterprise.'

The only problem with the indefinite extension of this scheme was that Charles was not alone in having seen its potential. He controlled four houses on Queen Street, but other, similarly ruthless, villains had control of the others. His attempt to seize a fifth house had resulted in his men receiving such a beating that one had lost the sight of an eye and another had lain close to death for a week. Sir Charles had, to his horror, received a visit at his home ('I don't know to this day how they found out where I lived') and the realities of the situation were explained to him. He could keep the four houses he had already in his possession, but if he were to attempt to gain control of more, the consequences would be severe.

'They say that life in the rookeries is lawless,' he told me, 'but there is law there. It is the Law of the Rookeries and it is enforced more firmly than ever the courts enforce the law in the rest of London.'

I nodded. It is said that nature abhors a vacuum and where the State holds no sway, then men will turn to other petty rulers who, having no prisons or machinery of law, will, perforce, deliver a cruder, more immediate simulacrum of justice.

Denied the opportunity to expand his new enterprise as a slum landlord, Sir Charles looked around for other possibilities. 'The pater had left things in rather a bad state. I needed the money.'

His tone was wheedling. Did he feel he needed to justify his crimes to me? Did he even seek my approval? It seemed safest to nod sagely and give him a hint of an encouraging smile. It took no more for him to continue with his tale.

Michael's account of his first days at Queen Street meant that the next part of Sir Charles' account brought no surprises. He had let out the better rooms to those, like costermongers, who had the means to pay the shilling or so he charged in rent. The cellars and some of the attic rooms, which a leaking roof had left barely habitable, sheltered those with no income at all. These men were set to begging.

'I'd have set the women to whoring, but any that were not too clearly poxed would have a protector who would find them shelter, so none of the bitches in my cellar could raise a penny from the sale of their bodies.'

I thought of how he could have forced Harry and Michael to raise money in this way but, fortunately, his mind ran only to conventional vice and this had not entered his imagination. Or perhaps he had feared the penalty of the law, which would be severe if he were caught procuring men for sodomy. In either case, my friend had been spared that.

'Begging brings in more than you would think.' As his sorry story continued, I realised that he was proud of his achievement. He was, in his own mind, of a part with every other Captain of Industry in the capital, building a business that might restore the fortunes of his family. 'But I soon realised that, with the men at my disposal, I could do better than begging.'

'You considered simple thievery.' I shouldn't have said it, I know, but I could not stop myself. He sounded more and more like the Chairman of the Board, congratulating shareholders on the way that their investment was growing. For a second, that twitch in his upper lip was back, and I wondered if I had gone too far. Sir Charles obviously thought that thievery was incompatible with his aristocratic heritage.

He hesitated in his narrative for a few seconds. Then the twitch subsided and he continued. 'Coining seemed a more suitable enterprise. I had the premises and I had the labour.' I noticed that he had skipped over the period when he was simply contracted to a coiner, passing out the products of another man's work and getting but a small proportion of the proceeds. Like many men of business, he dwelt more on his genius than the sordid details of his rise to success.

The rest I already knew. 'And now,' he concluded, 'I will be able to move to printing currency notes and our profits should grow substantially.' I noticed that it was he who would, in this account, be printing the notes. There was no more mention of my involvement than there had been of Michael's.

We had almost cleared the table of food by the time my host finally reached the end of his story. There was yet a plenitude of wine, and he poured generously while asking me to tell him a little about my life. He obviously thought it less interesting than his own, though, so I passed rapidly through my time in Borneo and India and concentrated instead on recent events in London. This let me move the conversation back to his own activities and what drove him to such lengths. Nothing he said led me to revise my opinion that he acted purely for mercenary reasons. He certainly had no involvement with the French being, in his own crude way, what he accounted a patriot. ('I'll wager you're glad to be away from India and those savages, aren't you, Williamson? England's the place to live. Best country in the world.') And when I mentioned the Communists he seemed genuinely to have no idea what I was talking about.

By the end of our meal, I felt I understood Sir Charles better, but nothing I had learned would help me in my dealings with the Home Office. Even at a more mundane practical level the meeting had not been as successful as I might have hoped. It turned out that Sir Charles, for all his boasted financial success, could not give me the crisp five-pound note I was so anxiously seeking.

I resolved the problem of the note the next day. I went to my bank and asked to withdraw money in the usual way, but said that I needed it for an elderly aunt who had an obsessive fear of dirt and disease. Would it be possible to have a new note? The clerk consulted with his supervisor and a brand-new currency note was procured, which was handed to me with profuse expressions of concern as to the welfare of my aunt.

With a model for him to work from, I could now set Mr Underhill to the task of engraving our printing block. Once that was produced – and he assured me that it would be the labour of but a few days – we would be ready to start work. The press had been installed in the adjoining house, one of the three others that Charlie owned, or, at least, controlled. There was not room for it alongside the coining and Michael saw no reason to stop the production of sovereigns simply because we would have the paper money.

'Having it next door is safer, anyway,' he said. I couldn't at first see why this should be the case, but he then explained his new arrangements. The steps to the cellar where the press was situated would be removed. The cellar door was locked and anybody breaking it down would fall to certain injury and possible death. We would have access through small openings that he was having made in the wall of the cellar we currently occupied. When I saw him explaining to his men where they were to remove the bricks I complained that the holes were ridiculously small – so low that you had practically to crawl through them.

'That's the beauty of it,' he explained. 'Anyone trying to get in is easily struck about the head by whoever is guarding the press. The police will think twice before they raid a place like this.' He grinned. 'It's a useful precaution against people we know, too. We wouldn't want our press to be acquired by any of the other gangs, the way we came by our coining moulds.'

Just in case there was a raid by the police, similar holes

were made in the opposite wall of what I now thought of as the Press Room. I was surprised by this, as the cellar next door was controlled by one of Sir Charles's rivals, but Michael assured me that such arrangements were common. Allowing the buildings to interlink made it much more difficult for the police to raid the rookery and it was understood amongst the inhabitants that it was in everybody's interests for such passages to be permitted. Rather to my surprise, these entrances and exits were never abused by other gangs, although they offered clear possibilities to anyone wishing to steal from their neighbours. People did steal from each other all the time, for it is a myth that there is honour among thieves, but the Law of the Rookery, which Sir Charles had told me about, was not a myth. Everyone in Seven Dials knew the advantages of being able to escape swiftly and silently should the police come hammering at the door. Anyone abusing the passages would, at best, face a beating and, at worst, be expelled from the community, which, for almost all of those living there, would mean a few sad weeks sleeping on the streets before nature or the violence of men brought their lives to an untimely conclusion.

While what I might call the 'legitimate' side of my criminal life was advancing straightforwardly enough, my 'illegitimate' work for the Home Office was making no progress at all and my nameless visitor was becoming increasingly threatening.

'If you cannot come up with evidence soon, we will raid the premises and take up all we can for forgery. If you are caught with the others, as far as I'm concerned that's also good. Your sodomite friends will be tried for buggery and dance at the end of a rope. If you're not in jail yourself, I hope you will be in the crowd to watch them.'

Time, it was clear, was running out. I needed to find some evidence that could get Sir Charles tried for treason, and I had only a matter of days in which to find it. Only in this way would I ever be free to return to Devon and go about my business unmolested.

If I did provide the evidence that the Home Office needed to bring Sir Charles to trial, it seemed likely that their agents would lose interest in Michael. Such, at least, is what I told myself, for otherwise I do not think I could have lived with my deceit. Surely even the most prejudiced spy could not believe that Michael was a foreign agent? His move to London was the first time that he had never been outside Bickleigh. No: the key to this whole absurd business was Sir Charles. He was, as far as the Home Office was concerned, a dangerous man. He was an aristocrat, albeit a minor one. His father had been an investor in the railway; he had owned property and had friends in the City. Sir Charles himself had benefited from a respectable education. Such men are the mainstay of British life. If once they turn on their own country, there can be no assurance of security for the nation. This, it seemed, was the way that the official mind worked, and I was not sure that there was not some truth in this reasoning. On such a basis, Sir Charles' treachery represented a real threat.

If I could link Sir Charles to a foreign plot – French or German, it really didn't matter – then I should be able to get Michael out unscathed. Of course, that meant saving Harry Price as well. I had no particular desire to do so: Harry was a nice enough fellow, but it seemed to me that he held Michael back. He was, and always would be, the product of a life of labour on the farm. Where Michael learned and soared in his new London world, Harry was content to make the tea and clean the room and watch over his lover like a mother hen with her chick. Michael was a fool to bind himself to such as Harry, but bound they were and I could not save one without the other.

But how could I implicate Sir Charles in a plot I was certain didn't exist?

CHAPTER EIGHT

While we installed the press and I bought paper and inks to match, as closely as we could, those used by the Bank of England, my mind was scarcely on my work. I worried at the problem all day and lay awake thinking about it half the night. And then, the evening before I was to collect the plate from Mr Underhill, I was accosted by a woman as I walked to my lodgings from Queen Street.

It was hardly an unusual occurrence, although many of the whores recognised me by now and left me alone. The woman stepped from the shadows with the usual nonsense about wanting company, only to shrink back as she saw my face. I recognised her a moment later.

'Mary!' For it was the maid that Sir Charles had dismissed.

'Sir.' She seemed filled with confusion and something like shame.

'Come, Mary,' said I. 'I have no need of whatever services you were planning to offer, but I will be happy to buy you a drink and, perhaps, something to eat.' I had scarcely met the girl before, but I was moved to offer charity because she appeared so distressed and painfully thin.

In the end, she took some coaxing before she would agree to accompany me to a nearby chop house. It seemed to me that her modesty was ill suited to her new trade and, as soon as she was sat down with food and drink before her, I asked how things had come to this.

'It was Sir Charles. He demanded … Well, you know how it is, sir.'

I did, indeed, know how it was. All I could do was nod and look sympathetic as the whole sad story unfolded. Sir Charles, like every baronet in every bad novel, had insisted on having his way with the poor girl and then, once he had tired of her, he threw her out on the street. With her history, and nowhere to live, the only alternative to starvation seemed to be to sell her body.

'After all, sir, it was no more than I had been doing with Sir Charles. But on the street it's different.' She choked back a sob.

I had intended to see her fed and to be on my way, but now it came to it, I did not feel I could abandon her. Was there not room for another body at Queen Street? Michael, after all, had found accommodation for Harry; why should I not be permitted to put Mary somewhere safe?

So, once she had eaten, I retraced my steps. Mary flinched a little as we entered Seven Dials. She clearly knew and feared its reputation, but she must have decided it was a better alternative to wherever she was sleeping now, and she followed close behind me as we made our way to Queen Street.

I marched up the stairs, skipping over the missing treads quite automatically, while Mary followed somewhat more cautiously. I knocked on Michael's door. There was a scuffling from inside and then it opened a crack and his flushed face appeared in the doorway.

'What are you doing here now, John?' Then, noticing the girl behind me, 'And who the hell is that? I hadn't thought you were the sort to be bringing a woman back here.'

Behind him, I could have sworn I heard Harry giggle.

'It's Mary, Michael. Sir Charles's maid.'

He peered into the gloom of the landing. 'Oh, yes. I recognise her now. What have you brought her here for?'

I explained how I had met her and that I felt I could not leave her on the streets and, eventually, reluctantly,

Michael agreed that she could stay.

'But she'll need to earn her keep and, from what you say, she won't be able to make money on her back.'

I said nothing, but let my expression speak for me.

Michael had the decency to look embarrassed. 'I'm sorry,' he said, 'but she will have to pay her way somehow.'

I smiled, for I thought she might be the key to solving my difficulties.

'Don't worry. I'll pay her rent. There's something she can do for me.' I heard Harry giggling again. 'And it isn't that.'

I went to see Underhill in the same Railway Arms where we had first talked. We greeted each other as if we had met by chance and we shared a pint before setting out to walk a little way together. He was wearing a coat, despite the warmth of the day and the reason for this became clear once we were alone on the street. He plunged his hands into the coat's capacious pockets and produced the plate that was the key to making our fortunes. It was carefully wrapped in cloth.

'You can unwrap it to check, if you want, but you shouldn't. You need to handle it carefully. It would be a shame to mark it after all the work I've put in.'

'No matter, I'll trust it's in there. I've brought half your money. I'll bring the other half once we've printed a test note and checked that it passes muster.'

Underhill gave me a tired smile, the smile of a man who has been so beaten down by life that he has passed far beyond complaining of his lot. 'It seems to me,' he said, 'that I'm trusting you rather more than you are trusting me.' It was true, of course. Once he had handed over the plate, he had no way of contacting me again, while I could easily locate him if his work was unsatisfactory. I had, though, some reassuring news for him.

'Don't worry, Jack. I won't run out on you. If this work is good, I have another commission.'

He looked at me, his visage showing equal parts of hope and concern.

'It's not more notes, is it? If we go above five pounds, we'll be caught for a certainty. They'll search us out and then it's Botany Bay and what happens to my children then?'

'No one will search you out for this,' I promised. 'It's the safest forgery you'll ever make.'

I had not intended to tell him then, but the worry on his face was so obvious that I decided to put him out of his misery.

'It's French money, Jack. I want you to forge me francs.'

Getting a clean French note proved surprisingly easy – much easier than getting the English five pounds. Despite the tension between the French and British governments, trade between the two countries continued and, where there was trade, there were people changing currency.

Foreign notes were generally treated less casually than British ones and, in any case, the fifty-franc notes had only been in circulation for a couple of years. In the end, I had a clean, crisp fifty-franc note before we had printed our first five pounds. Despite this, it was over a week before I was able to get back to Jack Underhill, who, by then, must have been convinced that I had vanished from the face of the earth, and his money with me.

The problem was not Underhill's plate. That, it eventually turned out, was of the finest workmanship. The difficulty arose with everything else.

We had thought that printing the notes would be a mechanical exercise well within the capability of the men working in our cellar. After all, they had produced coinage that had been passed across London with no difficulty.

They had even mastered the art of using electricity to plate the coins with gold. All they had to do now was to press an inky plate onto some paper and we would be the proud possessors of as much currency as we cared to print. We had paper, ink, and printing press. It could not, surely, be that difficult.

But Michael and I learned in the next few days that printing is not nearly as easy as one would imagine. The amount of ink on the plate is critical. Too little, and the image is faint, or in places non-existent. Too much, and the image is smudged. The curlicues that one takes for granted on a currency note turn out to catch ink between them. The design is not simply aesthetically appealing – it is purposely drawn to make it near impossible for an amateur printer to reproduce it.

Even with our first smudged and unusable attempts, it was also clear that the ink that I had so carefully matched did not provide exactly the same shade of black as was seen on a genuine note. I had realised that black ink is not all of a piece and had, I thought, carefully matched the density of the darkness in the ink that I purchased to that found on the note. However, a sample of ink scratched onto paper with a pen does not necessarily resemble exactly the shade that is produced when it is printed.

The paper, at least, proved to be exactly what we had hoped for, but even here we ran into difficulty. Each sheet had to be printed twice – once with a wire to press something that might be taken as a watermark and then again with the inked plate. Aligning the two presses took us a while, but we more or less managed. To be frank, by this stage of the proceedings, we just wanted something that bore enough resemblance to a real note for us to convince ourselves that what we were setting out to do was not totally impossible.

Finally, we had something that, in a poor light, might be taken by a man in a hurry to be a five-pound note. It had, of course, been printed in the centre of a sheet of paper that needed to be cut to size.

Michael duly attacked the paper with scissors. The results were not impressive: raggedy edges that bore no resemblance to the sharp sides of the genuine article.

For days we struggled with the press. Then Michael claimed he had the solution. The German Workers' Educational Society, he said, was always producing printed leaflets in their efforts to bring the ideals of Communist Germans to London. Surely one of these people would help us?

'They are no friends of the State, John, and they are the sworn enemies of bankers who represent the forces of Capital. Surely they would be happy to assist us in our enterprise? They can pursue their political ideals and make money at the same time!'

I could hardly believe what I was hearing. This was the very Communist plot that the Home Office had convinced themselves was already under way. If a printer from the German society were to be found on our premises, there was no chance of Michael escaping the rope.

I put every argument I could think of against the idea, but the trouble was that it was really a very good direction to pursue. Apart from their political leanings and the social class of the membership, the Communists seemed to have more than a little in common with the Masons. The members could rely on each other for assistance and they were bound by oath not to reveal their secrets to strangers. If their printer were approached, he would be unlikely to inform the authorities, even if he turned down the work. In part, this was because of the loyalty the comrades would feel to each other, but there was also the practical concern that, were they to inform the authorities, they would have to admit having been approached at a Communist meeting and most would be naturally unwilling to do so.

In the end, I suggested that we ask for help from Mr

Underhill. I argued that it would be wiser to keep to a minimum the number of people involved in the plot and that Underhill had already shown himself to be a very competent workman.

Michael was unsure. We didn't know Underhill; he lived too far away; he was nervous of breaking the law. I dealt with his concerns one after the other. Underhill, I convinced him, had involved himself so far with our plans that it would be no great effort to draw him further in. I would go and see him the following day, taking the remainder of the money we had promised for the engraving as evidence of our goodwill.

So the next day I made my way again across the river to Underhill's home. I did not warn him that I was coming, for I had no intention of meeting in public. I had delicate negotiations to conduct and Mr Underhill's own parlour seemed the best place to conduct them.

Although I had assured Michael that Mr Underhill would welcome the chance to join our enterprise, I was far from certain that this was true. Jack Underhill was, I thought, a fundamentally honest man, driven to criminality by desperation. With the money he made from the engraving and the promise of more once he had forged the fifty-franc notes, the threat of homelessness and hunger had receded. He might now decide to return to a respectable life.

It fell to me to make sure that he remained mired in criminality. I was not entirely comfortable with my role, but, after all, the money I was giving him would not last for ever. All I was doing was reminding him that he had a duty to his wife and children to earn as much as he could while the opportunity presented itself.

In the event, I did not need to deploy much in the way of persuasion. It seemed that engraving work had introduced him to the idea that crime does, indeed, pay, and he seemed to feel that, having become so intimately involved with the enterprise, he might as well see it through. He even quoted Shakespeare at me: 'I am in blood stept in so far, that should I wade no more, returning were as tedious as go o'er.'

Mr Underhill, it seemed, had depths I had yet to explore.

There was one issue that worried me and had, indeed, been the reason for not putting his name forward to Michael earlier. It was, I explained, absolutely essential that Michael did not find out about our arrangement regarding the francs. Underhill having access to the press at Queen Street meant that we should be able to produce the French money there, but it must be done in utmost secrecy and Michael must never know.

Underhill was uncomfortable with this idea. As I had foreseen, he was not by nature a dishonest man. The idea of concealing his activities from somebody who was by way of being his employer worried him, and I had to assure him that I was not attempting to steal from or damage Michael. 'It's an idea I want to try out,' I told him, failing even to convince myself. 'I don't want to share it until it's ready.' In the end, it was only because we had built some semblance of trust between us – a trust bolstered by the substantial sum I was paying for the francs – that he agreed to keep the French currency our secret.

I was able to return to Michael with a promise that Underhill would join us the next day.

Pleased as he was that we would have someone to work the press properly, I could tell that Michael was annoyed that I had preferred to use Underhill rather than approach one of his new friends at the Workers' Educational Society. It was understandable. Michael had been in charge of the coining operation and now I had come in and was favouring my own contacts over his.

I could hardly tell Michael the real reason for my

refusal to entertain the idea of using a printer associated, even tangentially, with the Communists. At the same time I did not want this to come between us.

Thinking about it, I decided that there was, perhaps, a way that I could include the German Workers' Educational Society in the plan that I was developing.

I started by apologising to Michael. I'd been nervous, I said. Maybe I had been hasty. It was just that I didn't know any of his new friends. Perhaps he could introduce me to the club and I could meet some of them.

Michael had never been one to nurse a grudge. In fact, he was delighted with my suggestion, though Harry, hovering as usual with tea and cake, shot me a very dark look.

I had no interest in the singing or the amateur dramatics, so, once Michael had been given approval to take a guest, I agreed that I would attend on a Monday. 'You'll be interested,' he said. 'You used to rule over the natives in the Far East, didn't you? So you'll enjoy talking about politics.'

In the end, it wasn't that bad. They were a decent bunch. Despite the cynical remarks of the gentleman from the Home Office, many of them were German. One or two even had the big black beards that cartoonists love to associate with German anarchists. Most, though, were quite nondescript, their shabby clothes revealing their status as refugees who had lost everything fleeing persecution in their own country. They tended to congregate in clusters around the room, speaking earnestly in German, but all smiled at me and one or two made little speeches of welcome in halting English.

The English men present (they were all men) seemed mainly to be artisans. I had the impression that these were people who, like Michael, were seeking self-improvement as much as revolution. In any case, though I had dressed in my Seven Dials clothes, they seemed instinctively to recognise my class and, far from attacking me as a bourgeois revisionist, they deferred in the way that artisans always do to gentlemen.

This was not an evening for a formal lecture – those were on Sundays – so people chatted informally about the burning issues of the day. The Englishmen were generally talking over pints they had brought up from the bar below. A few of the Germans were sipping uncertainly at their beer, but most seemed to be unwilling to experiment with the products of British breweries. Instead they drank coffee, prepared by one of their own who had established himself on a table at the rear of the room.

The main subject of conversation was Emperor Napoleon's defeat of the Austrians in Italy. There was much excitement and talk about how the peace had led to both France and Austria losing face. I must confess that the reasons for this escaped me, especially as they claimed that England and Prussia had lost out as well. One excitable little man was telling anyone who would listen that the only winners were the Russians and the revolutionaries, though there seemed no basis for this at all except, perhaps, wishful thinking.

After a while it became clear that the groups were not quite the casual conversationalists that they might at first appear. Earnest men with German accents were engaged with each of the groups of English members. From the snatches of talk that I heard, it seemed that they were definitely guiding the conversations.

One man, in particular, moved from group to group, engaging each in passionate conversation for a few minutes before moving on to the next. He, too, was bearded, though it was neatly trimmed and he was better dressed than many of the Germans. His hair was greying, but the beard remained dark, giving him a peculiarly distinguished appearance. He had rather a loud laugh which, in a room full of people talking seriously, drew attention to him. I listened as he moved to a group of English workers sitting near to where I stood with Michael, still taking in my surroundings.

I had no idea what he was talking about, but it obviously wasn't the French or the Austrians. 'Biskamp is a good enough fellow, but you mustn't believe everything he tells you. The paper's finances, for one thing, are in a terrible state.'

One of the men he was addressing put down his beer and seemed about to say something in favour of Biskamp – whoever he was – but the German interrupted.

'No, no, Wilkins. You will say that Biskamp has a fine understanding and that he writes the leader columns in *Volk*. But the man is a schoolmaster. I myself have had to find him a place in Edmonton. Edmonton!' He made Edmonton sound like Siberia. 'Believe me, he will not for long be writing the leaders.'

As he got more agitated, his accent became more pronounced, until he was scarcely comprehensible. The men he was addressing had obviously heard such rants before and sat quietly, as if waiting for the storm to pass. The German gave a final, incomprehensible, splutter of agitation and, looking restlessly about him, his eye fell on me.

I was, by now, quite obviously listening to the argument (if anything so one-sided could be called an argument), and the German immediately gave up on the group at the table and moved towards us.

'Michael.' All trace of agitation had gone and his accent was all at once less marked. 'You have brought a new friend.'

'Oh, yes!' Michael appeared quite flustered. 'This is John Williamson. John, this is Herr Doktor Karl Marx.'

We shook hands. Herr Marx's eyes sparkled with enthusiasm, presumably at the idea of having a new member to harangue.

'And what do you do, Mr Williamson?'

Before I could reply, Michael cut in, rather mischievously, I thought. 'John is in the printing trade, Herr Marx.'

'You are a printer!' Before I could respond, Marx had stepped forward to embrace me. 'But that is wonderful.' In his excitement, he pronounced it *vunderval*. 'I am needing a printer for my newspaper.'

'No, no!' I hastened to disentangle myself. 'I fear you do not understand. I am in the printing trade, but I am not myself a printer. Indeed, I have been looking for a printer myself.'

'Ach!' Marx released me from his embrace. 'So. It is ever thus. In London I struggle always to find a printer.'

'You are printing a newspaper?'

'Yes, the *Volk*. You would like to buy a copy?'

'Perhaps not at this moment.'

The poor chap looked so devastated at my rejection of his newspaper that I hastened to say something more positive. 'But there must surely be plenty of printers who would take on a job like that.' I thought of the men I had drunk with while I was looking for Underhill. 'I could recommend somebody, if you like.'

Marx grimaced. 'I am sure you would. And they would rob me. Mr Williamson, I am shocked by the prices that printers in London charge. And not only the presses that are owned by capitalists. No, even the printers who work for themselves, gaining a living from their own labour – even these men charge so much money. I do not understand it. Surely they should be proud to print for nothing ...' He checked himself. 'Well, maybe not for nothing. For the cost of their materials, perhaps.'

Having established that I was not in a position to print his newspaper, Herr Marx seemed to lose interest in me and with a nod he was off to another table.

Michael guided me to a quiet corner and vanished downstairs to get drinks. While he was gone, I was joined by an elderly man whose clothes, once fashionable, were now worn and somewhat out of style. He introduced himself as Mr Spencer.

'It's Dr Spencer, actually, but we British are not quite as fond of all these honorifics as our German friends, are we?'

I smiled as Spencer gave a half nod in the direction of Herr Doktor Marx. 'Actually, he's not a bad chap. I see him often in the Reading Room, working away at his *magnum opus*. He's quite convinced that he's going to change the whole way that we see the world and then we'll realise the error of our ways and the revolution will come.'

'He didn't seem particularly revolutionary.'

'No, he isn't. He's a scholar really. Tucked away in the suburbs with his wife and a cosy little housekeeper that people say is not just a housekeeper. He has daughters, you know. Lovely girls. I met them once.'

Michael returned with our drinks, and sat down to join us. He obviously knew Spencer and, after a few very English observations about the weather (it was still ridiculously hot), he asked him how his studies were progressing.

'Not too bad,' admitted Spencer. 'Not too bad at all. I've just got a copy of Mr Marx's latest effort.' He patted the pockets of his coat, eventually turning up a small volume which he placed on the table. *Zur Kritik der Politischen Oekonomie* was printed on the cover, above Marx's name, complete with honorific.

'You read German?' I asked.

'Have to, old chap. All the best stuff is in German.'

'Don't you worry that the authorities might act against you? Seditious literature or something?'

'Good heavens, no! This is England. We don't do that sort of thing.'

151

I thought of the man from the Home Office and wondered at the naiveté of the scholastic community. 'I rather think that if a man were suspected of something and that book were found in his possession, it might count against him.'

Spencer looked at me curiously. 'I suppose if you had a bomb in your suitcase, or some such. But I don't see that being a problem for me.'

The conversation moved on, but I felt that another part of my plan had fallen into place.

CHAPTER NINE

The next few weeks were busy. Underhill had got the press set up to his satisfaction and we had printed our first five-pound notes. The quality was excellent, although our inability to put a proper watermark into the paper continued to worry me. Still, once the notes were soiled and a couple of strategically placed creases had been added, they looked acceptable provided that they were not examined too carefully.

We had to develop a new way of passing off these notes, as I could hardly go about town casually spending five-pound notes in every shop I visited. The problem was that a five-pound note just made us too rich. What, after all, could you buy for five pounds? Certainly there were many things in life that cost more than that, but these were seldom cash transactions. Some, admittedly, were. I had heard, to my astonishment, that there were men who would pay as much as twenty-five pounds for the pleasure of the company of some courtesans for just twenty minutes or so. This, though, was of little use in passing off money. It was not as if the ladies in question could be retailed to others once we had purchased them with our forged notes.

It was as I was watching a funeral pass on its slow procession to Kensal Green that I thought of one way to turn bad money into good. The family following the hearse were all properly dressed in mourning and could have been almost any class of people, but their shoes gave them away. The battered leather and the worn soles were those of working people, who would have sacrificed much to make sure that their deceased relation was given a funeral that would reflect well on both the late lamented and his surviving kin.

In the midst of life we are in death. Funerals are a regular part of the lives of so many of us in this great city. They bring not only sorrow, but expense. And for the poor, on whom the expense bears most heavily, funerals are a particularly frequent visitor, the poor dying with greater regularity than the rich. Many workers, it is true, subscribe to one or another form of insurance, but for those who don't, the expense of a funeral is paid in cash. And with the cost of funerals being as high as it is, many a five-pound note would be passed to the undertakers.

Michael soon had his criminal army spreading through the poorer parts of town, seeking out the houses where crepe on the door knocker or drawn curtains showed that someone had just passed away. The man of the house would be shown a five-pound note and offered it for whatever coins they had scraped together for the funeral. We made no bones about the business. They knew they were buying false currency, but, faced with the sudden cost of death, most were prepared to take the risk. We discounted generously and the notes really were very good. It seemed reasonable to expect that the undertakers would not check too carefully when dealing with the bereaved – persons who would never have been associated with this kind of criminality. Even if they were taken up, we assured them, the courts would be likely to deal with them leniently, given the fact that theirs was a family in mourning. When I had come up with this plan, I had thought it a useful way to pass off a few notes, but I was surprised at how successful the scheme turned out to be. It was rare that anybody turned down the offer of discounted cash and I came to realise that for many poor people, a death in the family would mean weeks of hunger and cold until the damage to the household finances could be repaired. Of all the criminal acts which I have been forced to engage in, this was the one that gave me fewest qualms. It seemed to me that by relieving these families of some of this burden we were doing a good thing, rather than an evil one.

Generally, we passed on most of the notes by discounting them to people who were prepared to carry a risk. Publicans might reasonably have some five-pound notes from their business dealings, although they would never see a customer with that much money on them. There were plenty of landlords in the area of Seven Dials who were happy enough to slip one or two false notes in with their real ones, though they paid us only ten shillings for every five pounds we gave them.

So we gradually made more and more of the notes and found more and more people ready to pass them on.

Underhill would have been kept busy enough with his work in any case, for each note had to be exactly perfect and many were burned when he declared them flawed in some way or another. But when he and I were alone in the Print Room, he would remove the block with which we printed the five-pound notes and replace it with the plate for the French currency. Paper and inks would be switched and we would print fifty-franc notes. We could never produce more than two or three at a time, for they had to be left out to dry. We would conceal them behind the British currency, relying on the fact that the corners of the cellar were dark and neither Michael, nor any of his workers, had any reason to explore them. Even so, the secrecy with which we were manufacturing these extra notes made it a tedious operation.

'I still don't know why you're doing this,' Underhill complained one day. 'It's not as if you'll be able to use them in England.'

'No,' I said, 'I won't be able to spend them, but I'll find a use for them, sure enough.'

155

I'd gone to a couple more meetings of the German Workers' Educational Society and spent some time in conversation with Dr Spencer. I'd asked him about Marx's *Critique of Political Economy* and feigned interest when he explained it to me.

'It's not a particularly significant work,' he said. 'But it has some interesting ideas about interpreting history in terms of the underlying economic structure of society. Marx uses the word *basis* to reflect the underlying economics and *überbau* for the superstructure –'

'Ah, yes.' I interrupted before he could get carried away. 'It's such a shame that the work is not available in English. I have a friend who would dearly love to read it.'

Spencer's response came as no surprise, for he had talked a lot about the problems that he had encountered in translating the work. 'Why, I have a decent summary of the book in English. I'd be delighted to lend it to your friend if you would like.'

'That would be wonderful. Actually, he lives near here. Perhaps you could call on him with me after a meeting? I'm sure he would be delighted to meet someone who understands political theory as you do.'

They say that men are easily persuaded by a pretty face, but I find flattery is usually as effective.

All the elements of my plan were now in place. I just needed luck for me to be able to bring them all together.

Luck can, of course, be encouraged.

My plan required the man from the Home Office to call on me. He had always taken a cruel delight in refusing to give me any way to contact him, while turning up in my lodgings whenever he chose. Now I kept hinting that I was on the verge of a breakthrough and, combined with my failure to achieve anything so far, this meant that he was coming more frequently. I felt I had a good chance of seeing him as soon as the other parts of my plan were ready.

The next thing I needed to arrange was access to Sir Charles's house. Here I was relying on Mary's help – help she had been more than happy to promise me in exchange for a place to stay in Queen Street.

There was, as I had surmised, an excellent cook at the other Queen Street. Like all honest cooks – except in France, where honesty, in any case, can't be taken for granted – the cook was a woman. Her considerable culinary skills meant that Sir Charles did not dare molest her as he had Mary, but there was sympathy between the two women which the baronet's behaviour towards his maid had strengthened. When Mary had first been turned out of the house, it was gifts of food from the cook that had kept her from starving. 'Some nights, if Sir Charles was away, she snuck me in and I could sleep in my old bed,' she told me.

The news that Sir Charles was often away from home came as no surprise. Men of his sort are not known for regular domestic habits. I asked how Mary knew the nights that it was safe to visit her friend the cook.

'When Sir Charles is at home, the gas lights are left on in the front room. You can see the light through the curtains. He's never in bed before two, so if the light was off, I'd know he was out. Then I'd knock and Cook would let me in.'

Would the cook still let her in? Yes, she thought. Why not?

All was ready. The francs had been printed and I had a neat bundle of them secured with two of those new-fangled rubber bands. Dr Spencer was expecting to meet Sir Charles, and I was being visited by the man from the Home Office almost every day. Mary had called on her old friend the cook and persuaded her to give us the help we needed. If Sir Charles were out tonight, my plan could go ahead.

Michael had no idea of what I had in mind. It seemed safer that he should not know.

That night, I had agreed to go to Great Windmill Street with Michael. At the last moment, Mary said that she wanted to visit a friend nearby and asked me if I could escort her. 'It's just past Great Windmill Street. I'll hardly take you out of your way.'

Michael offered to accompany us, but I insisted that he go directly to his meeting and that I join him later. 'I won't have them say I'm making you late,' I told him. 'What would Mr Marx think of me?' He laughed, for Marx's outbursts of anger against those he thought lacking commitment to his ideals were famous. Some members had been driven out for failing to subscribe to his latest newspaper venture, while you risked banishment if you took the wrong side in the complex web of plots and alliances that seemed to envelop anything Karl Marx did. As a casual visitor, I was not drawn in to these concerns. Indeed, when Marx met me, he seemed to go out of his way to be charming and he also seemed well-disposed towards Michael: it was amongst the Germans that the in-fighting was most serious. Even so, it did no harm to stay on the right side of the Herr Doktor and Michael agreed that he would go ahead on his own and assure his friends that I would be there soon.

I gave a sigh of relief as Mary and I parted from Michael, only a few minutes' walk from the club. I had feared that he would change his mind and insist that we not walk on alone. It was still July, so there was no fog, but we had set out late and it was already dark and Michael was inclined to be over-protective of his friends. In this case, though, Michael's kindness was the biggest threat to our plans, for once we had left him, we hurried to Sir Charles' house. There, as we expected, no lights showed between the curtains drawn against the dark in his front room.

Mary knocked gently on the door, which opened, and she vanished inside.

I had crossed the road as we approached the house and I walked by it without pausing. If anyone were watching, I had no desire for them to notice me or to associate me with Mary. That there was someone watching, I took for granted. I no longer had any doubts about the existence of a secret police force in London and, for all that I despised the intelligence of my contact, there was no doubt as to the efficiency of their observational work. The fact that they would be keeping Sir Charles' house under observation, though, far from being a difficulty was a definite advantage for my plan.

I continued to the end of the street and then made my way back around the block to arrive at the Workers' Educational Society less than a quarter of an hour after my friend. I had an unpleasant shock at first, when I could not see Dr Spencer, but he arrived twenty minutes or so later, apologising for his tardiness. 'I got carried away with my translation work. I tried to find a hackney cab to make up the time, but there's never one when you want one, so I used the omnibus and of course it got stuck in traffic.'

I sympathised with him over the delays that had made him so late. I was still astonished every time that someone excused a delay by complaining of the traffic. After years abroad, the idea that the sheer volume of vehicles on the road could add significantly to the time taken for a journey seemed quite ridiculous. It was, though, the simple truth – although traffic delays at this hour of the evening were unusual. Dr Spencer agreed: 'I think that many carters are now bringing in goods at night, in order to avoid the worst traffic during the day. If this goes on, London will be enmeshed in stationary vehicles day and night.' At this point, Dr Marx joined us and we moved from a discussion of an implausible future for London's roads to the more realistic issues of the potential for revolution in Italy.

Marx was in an excellent mood – I heard later that he had been given some money to sort out the immediate problems of his newspaper – and his good humour infected the rest of us. So it seemed natural, at the end of the evening, that I suggest to Dr Spencer that this would be an excellent opportunity to call on my friend and give him the translations he had promised to lend him.

The evening was warm: it seemed that long, hot summer would never end. We needed no cloaks or greatcoats, but strolled out in our suits, enjoying the fresh air after the smoke and fug of the meeting. Michael headed straight back to Seven Dials, while Dr Spencer and I walked the short distance to that other Queen Street where Sir Charles lived.

This time I would not be able to avoid being seen by any watchers. Still, it was dark and, though the lamps had been lit in the street, gas-mantle light does not provide the best illumination. I would have liked to have covered my face with a scarf, but this would have been ridiculous in July, so I had to content myself with slanting the brim of my hat so as to cast my features into shadow. My suit was nondescript and could have passed for that worn by thousands of others. There was nothing distinctive about my appearance. I should pass without anything being noted that might identify me. Just to be on the safe side, I feigned a stumble as soon as we were out of sight of Michael. I gave a little yelp of pain and Spencer stopped in concern.

'It's nothing,' I said. 'Just twisted my ankle. I'll be all right.'

We moved on, more slowly now, for I took care to favour the leg with the ostensible injury. So, as I walked up to the door with my friend, I was confident that the unseen watchers noted only a stranger with a pronounced limp.

Our knock was answered by Mary. She had on her maid's uniform which Sir Charles had naturally kept when he evicted the poor girl. Of course, what the maid should have said in these circumstances was that her master was not at home and we would have left our calling cards and departed. Instead, she opened the door wide and asked us to enter. Any watchers would have had no doubt that Sir Charles had received a visitor.

Once in the hall, Mary apologised that the baronet was not in. Had he not remembered our appointment? Mary was embarrassed, I was embarrassed, and poor Spencer, like any good Englishman in an awkward social situation, sought to disengage himself as quickly as he could.

'It's no matter. I'll leave the papers here.'

I made as if to suggest he stayed but he was already turning to the door. 'No, no, I really don't want to be any trouble.'

He hurried out, so quickly I scarcely had time to call down the steps to him: 'I'll see you at Great Windmill Street next week.' I imagined the unseen watchers scribbling my words into notebooks. Mary and I caught each other's eye in the hall and found ourselves giggling uncontrollably.

I pulled myself together. Now was not the time to give way to silliness. 'Which is his study?'

'Upstairs. It's the first door on the left on the landing.'

We hurried up together.

I had worried that the study would have been bare of papers, Sir Charles not striking me as the studious type. To my relief, the desk was covered with envelopes, letters, bills and even a small packet which appeared to contain French postcards. All the better, I thought. Anything suggested a man of dubious morality was to the good and, though these particular photographs may not even have been produced in France, the association of this type of pornography with that country would do no harm.

I put Dr Spencer's notes on the desk, turning over the first couple of pages, to give the impression that somebody was in the process of reading them. My only concern was that, if Sir Charles came into his study, he might notice the papers and remove them. It seemed unlikely: the dust suggested that he could go for weeks without coming in. Still, to be on the safe side I moved a ledger on top of them. If Sir Charles did enter, he would find Spencer's work only if he looked through his papers immediately, and why should he do that?

The francs needed a little more thought. They needed to be hidden, but not so well hidden that they would not be found as soon as the place was searched.

There was a small bookcase against the wall opposite the desk. It was filled with the sort of thing that a cultivated young man was supposed to have read: Livy, Plato, a Bible of course, Shakespeare. There were some light modern works – Walter Scott featured prominently – and some books that a young man was definitely not supposed to have read. It was only these latter that showed any sign of recent use. *The Mysterious Mother* even presented signs of wear on the spine, but otherwise there was more evidence of dust on the bookshelves than on the desk. Sir Charles' failure to hire a replacement for Mary was leading to a drop in standards that were, I suspected, never too high to start with.

I pulled out a couple of the Greek classics, trying not to disturb the dust too much, and slipped the bundle of French notes in behind them.

It was as simple as that. Now all I had to do was to go home and wait for my visitor. I turned to Mary. 'Can you stay here overnight?'

She nodded. 'Cook says he won't be back until tomorrow.'

'Good girl.'

Mary opened the front door to show me out, every inch

the maid, and I set off to my own lodgings.

Once home, I did not have to wait long for the man from the Home Office. In fact, I didn't have to wait at all, for he had once again taken the liberty of letting himself into my room and sat on my solitary chair, reading a magazine. I thought I recognised *All the Year Round*, which surprised me as I would have thought it too satirical for his tastes. I couldn't be sure, though, for he put it quickly into a briefcase as I entered the room.

'Do you have any information yet?'

I again made a great play of taking off my hat, dusting imaginary dirt from it, and placing it on top of the wardrobe. 'Good evening to you, too. Do all the gentlemen at the Home Office lack the most basic civility?'

He drew his lips back from his teeth. I have seen such a look in Borneo when the wild Dyaks are preparing for war. It is not an expression I expected to see from a government official in London.

'I'm losing patience, Williamson. Do you have anything we can use against Sir Charles, or must we just be satisfied with your friends in Seven Dials?'

I sat myself on the bed and brushed more imaginary dirt from my trouser legs. I had been waiting for this moment and I intended to enjoy it for as long as possible.

'I believe Sir Charles had a caller this evening.'

My visitor, for once, looked quite impressed. 'How do you know that?'

'There was some talk at the German club.'

'Well, you're right, as it happens. It didn't make sense at first, because my men could have sworn he'd left for the night, but if he was plotting with the Germans he might have doubled back unseen.'

I was careful to keep my face blank. Let him imagine whatever story he wanted. I had only to sketch the vaguest outlines and his own greed for evidence of Sir Charles' perfidy meant he would fill in the details for himself.

'There was some talk of papers. Political papers.'

Really, it was like offering treats to a dog. He leapt up from his chair. If he had a tail he would have wagged it.

'Communist papers? From the German Workers' Educational Society?'

'I believe so. I only heard the tail end of a conversation.'

'I have him!' He paced the room, grinding his fist into his other palm. It was a very small room, so he could take only three paces, but he managed to give a convincing impression of energy and determination in each pace. 'I have him, by God!'

He reached for his hat.

'Wait.' I put my hand out to detain him. 'If you have Sir Charles, you don't need Michael Radford.'

He looked at me as if he had just discovered the source of a bad smell.

'I think Her Majesty's Government has bigger fish to fry than Michael Radford.'

Then he was gone.

I lay back on the bed, taking great breaths like a man who has just reached land after swimming through a tempest. The Home Office had its traitor and I could free myself from the embrace of their spies. I could return to Devon and take Michael back with me. And Harry, too, if that was what it would take to save my friend.

I would tell Michael in the morning.

The next day saw me make my way to Queen Street with an unusually enthusiastic stride. I even found a good word for one of the ladies of the night who had obviously extended her shift into the morning, and I tossed a penny to a beggar, though I knew that Charlie's toughs would be moving him on in an hour or two.

My good temper was not even spoiled when I arrived to find Michael berating one of his urchins for having stolen a spoon from one of his fellows. 'I don't care about all this "honour among thieves" malarkey,' he confided to me, 'but if they're stealing from each other, they're not stealing from the people who have the spoons in the first place.'

'So you'd have the workers show solidarity in their conflict with the bourgeoisie?'

Michael grinned. 'Or maybe I just want to ensure the best use of my labour by having each man perform a specialised task.' I recognised Adam Smith from my own studies and grinned back.

'So are you a capitalist or a Communist, then, Michael?'

'I'm a seeker after knowledge and self-improvement.' The boy was still there, clearly bewildered by our conversation. Michael bent forward and struck him soundly on the side of his head. 'Bugger off, you little scamp, and don't let me hear about any more nonsense like this.' Then, turning back to me: 'Did you and Spencer get over to Charlie's last night?'

'Yes. He was out, though.'

'No surprises there.' He began to fiddle with the connections on his electrical apparatus. 'There's not as much current as there should be. Perhaps I need to top up the acid.'

'Michael.' I touched his sleeve to bring his attention back. 'I need a word.'

'Hmmm.' He was still fiddling, poking at the contents of one of the jars with a wooden stick. There was a flash of light and a bang.

'Upstairs.'

He looked up from what he was doing, a flicker of irritation on his face. 'I have things that need doing here. Won't it wait?'

'Not really. No.'

'All right. Go on up and get Harry to make you a cup of tea. I'll join you in five minutes.'

I was going to argue. I didn't want a cup of tea and I didn't particularly want to spend five minutes talking to Harry, but he was already fiddling with the jars again, and I realised I was going to get nothing from him until he had finished.

I made my way up to his room. Harry opened the door with his habitual smile and I did my best to return it. I could not say why I did not really like Harry, but I didn't and I suspected that, for all his friendliness, he knew it.

'You look like you could use a cup of tea.'

I suppose it was in part his predictability. If Harry had ever had an original thought in his life, he seemed at pains to conceal the fact. I was never going to talk about either Karl Marx or Adam Smith with Harry.

'I'd love a cup, Harry.'

At least this got him out of the room while he scurried off to the kitchen to make a fresh pot. I sat myself at the table and filled my time planning exactly what I was going to say to Michael. I would tell him, I had decided, that one of my investments in India had suddenly returned a handsome profit on my speculation. My fortunes restored, I would be able to leave London and even have a little spare capital to invest in a business. Michael, I was sure, would be more than happy to leave a life of crime in Seven Dials behind him, if he could establish himself in legitimate employment elsewhere.

Harry bumbled back in. 'I brought some biscuits, too. Got them from a new place in Covent Garden – very nice.'

Harry might be more of a problem. But it wasn't as if he worked. He could follow Michael anywhere, and would presumably be glad to get away from the filth and squalor of his present life.

I watched as he set out his tea service. Since I had first taken tea with Harry he had acquired a milk jug to match the cups and plates. 'Shall I be mother?'

I nodded and he poured, a picture of domestic

happiness. I began to have a nagging doubt about whether he would necessarily share my view that anywhere would be better than Seven Dials.

We sat in a slightly awkward silence, punctuated by remarks about the weather. Ten minutes passed; then fifteen.

'He gets carried away in his work,' said Harry.

I nodded. With every passing minute I felt less and less confidence about the way that our meeting was going to go.

By the time Michael finally appeared I was tense and annoyed. Perhaps things would have gone better if I had not been.

'So now you have money again, you are going to lord it over the likes of me!'

Harry had fled, ostensibly to make some more tea, and now I was alone with Michael, who was as angry as I had ever seen him.

'I've made something of myself here. I'm respected. I have a position.'

I should have kept my temper. I know I should. Does the Bible not say, '*A soft answer turneth away wrath: but grievous words stir up anger*'? But Michael's fury roused my own ire.

'A position! A petty lordling in a realm of thieves, and grovelling in your turn to that wretched creature, Sir Charles Crawley.'

'Good God, you're jealous! You see Sir Charles, with his title and his family, and you know that you can never be the man he is, for all the years you spend playing at being king over a bunch of savages.'

We stopped, both silenced by the venom in our own words. We half stood, leaning forward on the table and breathing heavily like men who had just been in a fight.

It was at that moment that Harry returned with the tea.

Perhaps he had been listening at the door, waiting for a moment of calm.

'Are you two boys quarrelling?'

It was like being scolded by a disappointed parent. I said nothing. I had been a fool and my plan was now in ruins.

'John says we should leave.' Michael spoke flatly, as if his anger had burned out. Harry's response, though, was furious enough for two.

'You think we should leave!' He had slammed the tea down on the table so hard that I had feared for the pot. 'And where would we go?'

'I can help.' I was almost stammering in the face of such antagonism, and from a man I had scarce heard raised his voice before. 'We could all go back to Bickleigh. I can set you up in business.'

'You can set us up! In Bickleigh!' His voice dripped contempt. 'In Bickleigh, where I was beaten by the other boys because I was not as manly as them? In Bickleigh, where the minister preaches that anything outside his own experience is a vice? You are going to set Michael and me up there? To live for a week or two before we are taken before the court and sentenced to hang?'

He stopped, his outburst over almost as soon as it had begun.

There was a long silence. Michael rose from his seat and went and put his arm around his friend. I sat, contemplating my own stupidity.

I had been able to live with James in Borneo, because he ruled the country. So long as we were discreet, no one would question our behaviour. In India, Mungo had explained to me that people understood that a man might love a man. He was a noble and lived in a palace. No one would dare to accuse him of any crime. But Michael and Harry were farm workers, whose homes had been tiny cottages in a village where everybody knew everybody else's business. In England, what they did in their bed was a capital offence. Church and State condemned it and their neighbours would condemn it too. Only in Seven Dials, in what I had, until that moment, considered a pit of immorality, only there had their love been able to flourish.

Still not speaking, Harry poured tea, the universal panacea of the English. He pushed a cup towards me and I picked it up and drank.

Nobody said anything until they had drained their cups. Then, before anyone else broke the silence, I said, 'I'm sorry.'

Harry reached across and patted my hand. 'I don't suppose you really thought about it.'

I understood in that moment why Michael loved him.

'I'm sorry,' I said again. 'There's something you have to know.'

My tone must have warned them. There was no trace now of the anger that had dominated the room, just a quiet tension while they waited to hear what I had to say.

'Sir Charles has been taken up by the police. You need to leave.'

There: it was said.

Only, of course, that was the very start of things. How did I know, asked Michael and, tired of the lies and deceit, I told him.

I think that all that stopped him from killing me straightaway was that the scale of the betrayal was too great for it to sink in. As it did, he rose from his chair, standing between me and the door.

Again, it was Harry who stepped forward to make peace. 'Michael. I think he was trying to protect you.'

Michael stared at me, as a man might stare at a demon suddenly walking beside him.

'Harry's right,' I said. 'They knew. They were going to take you up. Harry too. They said they would spare you if I gave them Sir Charles.'

For a long time he stood, staring at me. Then, slowly, he sat himself down again. 'So we're safe.'

I shook my head. 'They are going to charge Sir Charles with treason.' Michael stared at me in shock. 'It's nonsense, but they will. They'll say the press is a foreign plot.'

Michael began to protest, but I cut him off. 'It's nonsense, Michael. It's all politics, but that's what they'll say. But they'll need to produce the press.'

It took him only a moment to realise the implications and then he was starting down the stairs. I was just behind him as he arrived in the cellar.

'Smash the moulds!' He was shouting to the men sat at their workbench. 'Now! Smash them!'

It took a moment for the command to sink in, but then the sharpest of the men was smashing the plaster moulds on the floor, grinding them with his heel.

'How can that help?'

I did not realise I had spoken aloud until I heard Harry answering my question. I turned in surprise, for Harry never came down to the cellar.

'They need the moulds to prove coining,' he said. 'Without them, they can prove possession of the coins but there's no actual evidence that we made them.'

'I think there are enough coins to act as evidence by themselves,' I said.

'The law's a funny thing,' said Harry. 'But I trust Michael. He'll know how to get us out of this.'

As he spoke, Michael was grabbing handfuls of the coins and carrying them to the electrical apparatus in the corner. Turning, he saw us watching and shouted across the growing chaos in the cellar. 'Get the tin into the acid.'

I grabbed handfuls of counterfeit coin myself and joined Michael in dropping them into the jars. There was a lot of fizzing, and smoke rose from the apparatus. Acid splashed from the jars, burning fresh marks into the wooden bench.

Now people were rushing to and fro: some hurrying to destroy evidence, while others were already climbing the steps, anxious to be out of the way now it seemed that the police might be coming. The confusion was added to by the poor light in the place. In the panic one of the oil lamps was knocked over. Fortunately, it went out without catching fire to anything, but it left the place still gloomier.

Michael called across the room. 'Get John-John down here.'

From the top of the stairs, somebody called for this John-John and a few seconds later the giant from the hall was barrelling down the steps, casually pushing anyone in his way back to the cellar floor. I realised I had never asked his name. The fellow did not generally show himself. His job was to lurk in the shadows near the door and stop any unwanted visitors. It was not a position that called for sociability and I had never had cause to speak to him after my first visits.

'Get into the next room and barricade it. Get some of the others to help you.'

'You! You! You!' The giant pointed to the three nearest men who abandoned their hopes of fleeing and scurried through the hole connecting the main cellar to the Press Room. If John-John asked for your help, you didn't argue.

'Any of the rest of you who want to leave, get out now. There's a shilling for each of you that stays.'

There was movement in the shadows at the bottom of the stairs. A few men headed up, but most turned back towards Michael. People will do a lot for a shilling in Seven Dials.

'Take all the rubbish you can find and pile it against that wall.' Michael pointed at the opening to the Press Room. Then, shouting through the hole: 'Are you all right in there, John-John?'

171

'All well here. Can I take this great thing for a barricade?' He was talking about the press – the engine of our enterprise and the key to our fortune. I saw Michael's features twist with emotion for a moment, but he scarcely hesitated. 'Yes. It's the heaviest thing in there, and if the police find it, we've lost it anyway. Is Underhill in there with you?'

John-John confirmed that he was.

'Send him out. Tell him to bring the plate with him.'

There was a short pause and then Underhill, visibly frightened, emerged with the five-pound note plate in his hands. To my relief, I saw that, even in his panic, he had thought to conceal the plate for the francs in one of his capacious pockets.

Michael spoke quickly, keeping his voice reassuring. 'We're not going to be able to destroy it. And, in any case, Underhill, it's splendid work.'

Terrified as he was, Underhill still managed the ghost of a smile at Michael's praise.

'Get out of here and go home. No one here except John knows your address. You should be safe there.'

Underhill nodded and ran for the steps. I prayed he got away. Most of the inhabitants of Seven Dials were habitual criminals and expected occasional spells of imprisonment, but Underhill came from a respectable trade. He had a decent home and a wife and child. Imprisonment would destroy him.

From the other side of the wall came a great crash as the press was turned over, and I heard it scrape along the ground as John-John pushed it up against the entrance. Michael was already directing men to pile rubbish up, hiding the hole.

'What about the other entrance?' I asked.

Michael shrugged. 'It's two houses away. If the police are on their way, we have to worry about this one. We'll hope they don't search that far down the street. Are you absolutely sure they know this address?'

'Every time I visited, they knew. They must have the place under observation.'

'Well, we can put a stop to that, in any case.'

Most of the younger boys had gone, but a few were smashing the glass jars at one end of the room or helping pile up rubbish at the other. Michael beckoned two over.

'Have you seen anyone you don't know hanging around?' Both shook their heads and Michael looked at me. In that light, it was difficult to see his expression, but I knew he would be wondering if I had made a mistake.

'Lads,' I said, 'is there anyone who has arrived in the past couple of months?'

Now they nodded. There were a few. 'Half-a-dozen fellows, like,' the older boy volunteered. 'They turned up weeks ago and they're always coming and going. We asked them who they was and one of them said it was none of our business and threatened to clip us round the ear 'ole, but the other said they was just down on their luck and passing through. He 'ad some raspberry drops and he shared them with us.'

'Are any of them around now?'

'Bound to be. There's always a couple about.'

'Can you point them out to me?'

We slipped upstairs and watched from a window as the lads crossed the road and started to chat to two of the idlers who kept regular station along the streets of Seven Dials, so much a part of daily life there that another two attracted no attention.

One of the men, tall and dark, produced a bag of sweets and handed one to each of the boys. The other, a swarthy chap with a broken nose, turned away, apparently indicating that he wanted nothing to do with them. The boys moved off down the street, shouting thanks to the first of the two spies and muttering (presumably) imprecations about the other.

173

'We'll crack their heads at any rate,' Michael grunted.

'Why bother?' I asked. 'It's not as if they can do any more harm now.'

Had I known what was to happen, I'd have killed them myself, but, as it was, Michael grunted again and we returned to supervise the destruction of the cellar.

CHAPTER TEN

'There's coppers coming!'

The cry went up from a score of children's throats. The urchins of Seven Dials were doing what they did best: keeping watch on the streets and warning of danger.

'They're coming from Holborn!'

'They're coming from Covent Garden!'

Now men's voices were joining. 'It's a raid! It's a raid!'

There were all sorts and conditions of people living in Seven Dials: thieves, robbers, whores, confidence tricksters, bookies. Most were criminals of one sort or another, but there were those who found a living on borderlines of legality: publicans, crossing sweepers, costermongers. All were united, though, in their hatred of the police. The police took up the criminals, raided the bookkeepers, and persecuted the costermongers. To the inhabitants of Seven Dials the police were, simply, the enemy. And now the enemy was marching in force into their world.

'Stay inside! But move along the street.'

Now the warren of tunnels and passageways that linked so many of the houses came into its own. We slipped through cellars and vanished into cupboards to emerge in the next house. We zigzagged our way up and down stairs until we came to a room that looked out over the street. Michael crossed quickly to the broken space where a window had once been and, carefully raising his head above the sill, looked down to the cobbles below.

He beckoned me to join him and I saw we were now

some way along the terrace.

'Your friends must be really anxious to find this press.' I could hear the bitterness in Michael's voice. I understood how he felt. I had acted for the best, but what I had done must still have seemed a betrayal.

Three floors below us, the tramp of police-issue boots drummed a steady beat on the cobbles of Queen Street.

I think there were fifteen of them – five rows marching three abreast. Their blue uniforms looked smart enough and the tall hats that they wore to make them visible in a crowd gave an almost dandyish air to their appearance, but the truncheons left no doubt as to their willingness to fight. They marched like an invading army and, from inside the crumbling tenements, the men and women of Queen Street prepared to defend their territory.

The trouble started when they were less than a quarter of the way up the street. From the windows high above them, a rain of missiles began to fall on the police. People threw whatever they had to hand. Most in Seven Dials had few possessions they could casually discard, so what they mostly threw was the rotting fabric of the houses themselves. Bricks and pieces of wood crashed onto the street. I saw one policeman fall and his comrades pull him into what they thought of as the safety of a doorway. Moments later they were back on the street as men armed with clubs and knuckledusters smashed their way out of the building, laying about them in a paroxysm of violence. As the police turned from the road to protect their own, the ruffians vanished back into the house. Some of the police went to follow them, but the sound of an officer's whistle called them back into their ranks. Slowly, carrying their wounded with them, they started on along the street.

Harry had followed us and now he, in turn, peered out of the window.

'They'll not get through,' he said.

'You're forgetting the ones coming from Covent

Garden.'

As we watched, another policeman fell, but his comrades just picked him up and carried him on down the street. I heard an order shouted and the blue-coated figures began to trot, dragging their wounded between them.

'They're just going to run the gauntlet,' said Michael, a reluctant admiration in his voice.

I watched as if it was all something happening far away, nothing really to do with me. I heard the shouted orders and the screams of a wounded man and for a moment I was back in Borneo, watching Keppel's troops hack their way through a native village. 'If they want to stop them, the people will have to take to the street.'

'No. People will be beaten down in the open, and if the police can't get through, they'll call out the yeomanry. They'll get through to the house, but once they're inside, we'll have them.'

I thought of the fighting in the dark corridors of the Cawnpore barracks, the feel of a body struggling in the dark, the warmth of blood as a knife went in.

Michael turned and shook me. 'Are you all right, John? You look as if you've seen a ghost.'

'I'm fine.' I had seen a ghost, though. Thousands of ghosts. Makota, falling to the ground, his executioner wiping his blade; Mungo lying on the floor, his neck broken; the women falling to the rifles of the rebels in Wheeler's wretched Entrenchment. So many bodies, so much blood. I had thought I had left this violence in the Far East. I had believed it to be part of the business of ruling men who did not share our civilisation. Now, below me, I watched the police bleed and fall and soon they would be fighting in the passages and corridors that made the rookery as much a fortress as a home.

Michael was not reassured. 'You should get out of here. Take Harry and run. It's not your fight.'

'It is though. I'm the reason they're here.'

They had reached the door to the house where the coining operation was run. One of the spies the boys had pointed out to us came forward and pointed. I heard orders shouted and the police gathered round, ready to break down the door.

'Bastards. We should have killed them while we had the chance.' Michael stared balefully as the spies apparently gave directions to the officer leading the police. 'It will take a while to get in, at any rate. We've barricaded that hallway. No one will be getting through in a hurry.'

The barrage of missiles from the upper floors had eased off. People inside the house were preparing for a fight. I knew they would be lurking behind doors, hiding in the shadows, ready to strike down the forces of Queen Victoria's law that had dared to invade their domain. Any missiles would be saved to drop down stairwells.

We could hear the shouts and the crash of bricks and stones coming from the West now. I risked leaning out and saw the head of a second column of police arrived at the other end of Queen Street. They were moving fast and seemed to have dodged most of the missiles thrown at them.

At what I thought of as 'our' house, the group of police had parted, allowing two of their number to take a run-up at the door. Both crashed their shoulders into the wood at the same moment, but there was no sign of it giving way.

'I must get back there.' Michael was already heading for the door. 'You should leave, John. Take Harry.'

'I'm staying with you, Michael.' Harry spoke with unaccustomed firmness.

'For God's sake …' Michael turned to me. 'Please say you're going to be sensible.'

I shook my head. 'I'm afraid you're stuck with both of us, Michael.'

'Well, make sure you keep up then.' And then he was off, along secret ways and hidden passages until we emerged into the hallway where I had first met John-John.

Everybody had had plenty of time to leave and Michael was not promising them money, even if he'd been in a position to pay them, which looked increasingly doubtful. Yet the house seemed full of people, waiting and listening as the front door crashed to the blows of the policeman's shoulders.

The door was, indeed, well barricaded. The hallway was filled with furniture piled up to block the entrance. John-John was adding to the pile, flinging around tables, chairs, and assorted domestic debris as if they weighed nothing.

'Nobody is going to get in here for a while, lads.' Michael moved into command, the men naturally deferring to him. 'Is there still a fire in the kitchen?'

There was, it seemed.

'And any water?'

Yes, a churn full of water had been carried to the kitchen that morning.

'Boil the water, carry it up the stairs, open the window and give the coppers a bath.'

There was laughter in the hall and a couple of the men vanished into the kitchen to carry out their instructions.

I edged close to Michael and spoke softly. 'This is madness, Michael. Just get everyone out. You can – there's still time.'

He looked at me but made no reply, instead raising his voice so that everyone could hear him. 'They'll get in eventually, boys,' he said, 'and then there will be heads broken. Who's for leaving now? I'll not think the worse of you.'

There was a resounding cry of 'No!' which seemed to be joined by every soul in the place.

'It seems they want to stay, John.' Michael raised a quizzical eyebrow. 'And you too, apparently, for all that I've told you to leave.'

He looked round again and then turned to one man standing half way up the stairs. 'You, Paul Ashworth!'

'Aye.'

'Your wife gave you a daughter last week.'

The man drew himself up, pride shining from his dirty face, for all that his clothes were patched and his hat was dented.

'You have a room in Dudley Street.'

Ashworth nodded.

'Then take yourself off to her. Your child needs you more than I do.'

Ashworth protested, but Michael would have none of it, and the man was forced to climb the stairs to make his way through the warren to where he could appear safely on the street and return to his wife and child. As he went, his fellows slapped him on the back with every sign of sympathy. It is a strange force that makes us fight for the places that we call our own, even when it is a fight that we are doomed to lose. I had spent but a few weeks in Seven Dials and thought it one of the worst places in the world. Until that day, I would have given much to shake its filth from my feet. Now, with the police beating at the door, I stood alongside the men I had come to think of as, if not friends, then comrades. Here we would make our stand. England had given the people of Seven Dials nothing but these stinking streets and these squalid slums. Little as it was, it was all they had and they prepared to defend it against an invader who had already robbed them of everything else.

There was a sound of water splashing outside and screams showed that at least some of the constables had been burned. Inside there was a mocking laugh.

The violence of the blows on the door increased. From the sound of it, the police had found a baulk of timber or something similar, and were using it as a ram. As I watched, I saw the first splits in the door, as the wood began to splinter under the relentless battering.

Now there were gaps in the wood large enough to peer through. Inside mocking jeers greeted the sight of the police who, seeing the blockage in the hall, drew back from the door. More jeers and laughter followed, cut off suddenly as a crash outside revealed that the police, having given up on the door, had broken in through the ground-floor window.

'Some of the bastards must have cut the bars while the others beat at the door,' someone said. The news was greeted with a sullen silence as we listened to the tramp of feet in the front room. All was not yet lost. The debris that filled the hall blocked the only door the police could enter through. It was not as solid a barricade has had prevented them entering through the front, but I hoped it would hold them up for a while. What I had not allowed for was the sheer number who were now engaged in trying to enter the house. About a dozen of those we had seen arriving were still in a condition to fight and they had been joined by the men who had come up from the other end of the street. Thinking about it, there were probably more than twenty police beating their way in.

The door from the front room opened and blue uniformed figures began to tear at the jumble of furniture blocking the hall. The barrier that had so effectively held back the police now worked to their advantage, blocking attempts by Michael's men to attack them. Missiles were as likely to smash into the barricade as to strike their intended targets. Yard by yard, the police forced their way in. As they did so, they cleared away the obstructions that blocked the front door and all too soon the hallway was a mass of uniformed bodies.

'Now the game begins in earnest.' Michael seemed to relish the challenge that the police now presented. They ignored the door to the cellar, but pushed forward. We fell back, fleeing up the stairs, apparently in disarray. The police ran in pursuit but, in the shadows, they soon found themselves stepping into emptiness where the treads had been removed. Now our men turned on them. Table legs made crude clubs that beat upon the fallen police. Soon the constabulary were back at the foot of the stairs to the jeers of the locals. No longer protected by the barricade they had broken through, the police were subjected to a barrage of missiles thrown from above.

For a few minutes I thought we might have achieved an easy victory, but the inspector leading the police was no fool. He had his men take one of the battered doors from what remained of its hinges and, holding this above their heads to protect themselves, they began to move up the stairs again, cautiously testing each step.

Again, our men fell back. What else could they do? There was a strategy in their withdrawal, though. As the police pursued them into the house they were being drawn further from the cellar. Also, although they seemed to be having the better of the fight, their number was being slowly but surely reduced. Two of the men attacked on the stairs would not be joining in the fray for some time. Of the thirty or so men who had entered Seven Dials I doubted that more than twenty were still fit for duty. There seemed a real possibility that they would withdraw before they discovered the first cellar, let alone the Press Room. If we could drive them out today, who knew how long it would be before the police ventured into the rookery again?

Once upstairs, Michael's forces divided. Some vanished into bedrooms where wardrobes disguised doorways to other houses; some ran further to the next floor. The police, too, scattered, some breaking open the doors on this floor, others heading up the stairs. Michael was one of those moving upward and Harry and I followed him. It was easy to stay ahead of the police, for they still had to tread carefully to avoid the traps offered by the missing treads while we skipped over them with the speed of long familiarity. On the top landing a ladder led to a trapdoor that would take us through to the roof space. We were up the ladder and had pulled it after us before the first policeman had made it to the landing. I caught a glimpse of his face, red with anger, his features twisted in frustration as he saw us disappear.

We scurried along the planks that gave safe passage, easily seeing our way as light streamed through the holes where slates were missing from the roof. Once, I missed my step and put my foot through the plaster of the ceiling below. Michael laughed. 'I think that may be Roland's room. Charlie was saying we should charge more for that place. I'm not sure he'll be able to now.'

We arrived at another trapdoor and Michael opened it, dropping lightly to the floor below. Harry and I followed rather less elegantly and started down the stairs. This house was quiet, though sounds of battle could be heard faintly from the direction we had come.

We hurried down, taking care not to get caught by the missing treads. It was apparently a trick used in most of the houses hereabouts but the pattern of absent treads was unfamiliar to us, so we needed to proceed with caution. Even so, it only took a couple of minutes before we were carefully opening the front door. Ahead of us, the street was empty, but to our left the crowd had gathered to abuse the police. The odd cobblestone was being thrown, to little effect as the crowd was outside the house and the police were, by now, all sheltered within.

'Pathetic,' muttered Michael, as much to himself as to us. 'Herr Marx will be waiting a long time to see the English rise in revolution if this is the best they can do.' Even as he spoke, Michael was striding down the street towards the crowd. Arriving, he started to harangue them with a rhetoric that Marx would have been proud of. Were they not workers? Was it not their labour that had built this country? And were they now to stand by while the agents of state repression drove them from their homes?

Some of the faces that turned to him were visibly confused by a style of rhetoric that had not been heard before in Seven Dials. I was confused myself, for, German Workers' club or not, he was hardly a revolutionary. It was only later that I realised why he was fighting so hard in a lost cause – for surely we must both have known the cause was lost. Yet, like the rest of the mob, I was stirred by his speech. The political sentiments may have confused us, but there was no mistaking what he wanted us to do – and once they had a leader the mob was easily persuaded to join the battle inside the house. Michael, of course, was at the fore and I was swept along with him.

I had entered through that door and climbed the stairs dozens of times in the past few weeks, but now the place was utterly unfamiliar. I clambered over the debris in the hall and started up the steps, trying to ignore the blood pooled here and there. The fighting was above us now, but as we emerged on to the first floor we were caught up as bodies smashed in and out of doorways. All around, it seemed, men struggled and swore, their cries punctuated by the sound of truncheons on flesh and the crack of knuckledusters against bone.

For the next half-hour we roamed through the houses, for the police, too, were now using the corridors and doorways that linked them and the battle carried on continuously across three or four separate dwellings. I stayed close to Michael, with Harry constantly at his side. Unlike me, he knew where sections of floorboard had been removed so that a pursuer who stood carelessly on the apparent security of a rug might fall to the floor below, to be rendered *hors de combat*, possibly for all eternity. At least those who fell from the upper floors met a clean end. In the cellar of one of the houses, a tarpaulin had been stretched across the unemptied cesspit. As we carefully slipped past it in the dark, breath held against the smell, a frantic splashing in the filth revealed that at least one constable had fallen into the trap.

Here and there we would pass the prone figures of those combatants no longer able to raise fist or weapon against their enemies. An unspoken truce protected these men from further harm: a fellow in his blooded working clothes would lie gasping alongside a casualty in the uniform of the Metropolitan Police while the fighting passed them by.

I lost track of time in the chaos of the battle – for battle it was. Thirty minutes had passed, or perhaps an hour or more, when there was the sound of police whistles from room to room and suddenly the enemy was giving ground.

'They're pulling out!' Michael's amazement was as obvious as his delight. 'We've won!' He turned and embraced Harry in a huge bear hug. 'We've bloody won!'

But we hadn't.

The police hadn't left the building. They'd simply given up on the futile task of chasing men who knew the warren much better than them and done what they should have in the first place. They'd found the cellar.

Michael should have walked away. He'd put up a good fight and there was nothing to be gained now. Yet he couldn't. That cellar and the secrets it concealed had been the making of him. It was only now that I realised that the Michael who had left Bickleigh had gone. The farm labourer was replaced by a leader: cunning – ruthless, even, when he had to be – and trusted by the men around him. In Seven Dials he had found respect and even love. He should have walked away, but he couldn't.

The police had fallen back to the hallway of the house, where they left a goodly number of men to defend the entrance to the cellar. Michael's plan was to gather his forces and then move into the hall with around half coming downstairs. The other half were to leave one of the houses further along the street and then attack through the front door. He reasoned that an assault from both directions could let them drive all of the constables into the cellar, where they would be trapped.

It was useless my trying to point out that this would hardly be an end to things. It was not as if the Commissioners of the Metropolitan Police would allow us to hold them off indefinitely. Michael did not care. His blood was up and all he wanted was to see the police beaten.

It took a while for us to gather everyone together, for the fighting had split up our forces, just as it had those of the police. There was plenty of time, though, for, having discovered the cellar, the constabulary seemed in no hurry to depart. We agreed our strategy: John-John was to lead the charge down the stairs, while Michael brought the second group in through the front door.

Harry and I stayed with Michael and were at his shoulder as he burst out of the house next to ours and into Queen Street.

That was when it all went wrong.

The police had sent for reinforcements – only half-a-dozen men, but it was our bad luck that they had just arrived and were waiting outside as we emerged. We should have turned and fled back into the building, but we outnumbered them and Michael was doubtless driven on by the fact that John-John would be relying on us.

We set on them with a roar, but, in the open, they had the measure of us. An inspector was with them, shouting instructions, but Michael was urging his men on too and the fight could have gone either way. At that moment, though, I saw the man with the broken nose say something to the inspector and point towards where I was standing next to Michael.

There were shouted orders, impossible for me to make

out over the noise of the crowd, but then the police began to battle their way towards Michael.

Everything seemed to happen very slowly. I saw truncheons rise and fall. Men clutched at their faces, blood streaming through their fingers. A space opened up around Michael. Suddenly Harry and I seemed to be the only ones left standing anywhere near him.

'Not him! The other one!'

I could hear what the officer was shouting now. He pointed towards Michael and a constable who had been heading in my direction veered off. There were blue uniforms between me and my friend. Only Harry stood beside him now and he threw himself forward, desperately trying to get between the police, their truncheons pummelling down on him, and his lover. Michael was on his knees, but still holding his head upright as Harry moved to protect him. A truncheon blow aimed at Michael's body fell instead on Harry's head. He collapsed forward and the other police struck out at him, impatient to force him aside from their target.

I clawed at the blue uniform in front of me. I had to reach Harry and Michael. He raised his truncheon and I braced myself for the blow, when I heard the man with a broken nose speak. 'Get him out of here. We don't want him hurt.' Arms in thick blue cloth wrapped themselves round me and two constables dragged me away from the fight. The man with the broken nose followed.

The police deposited me, none too gently, on the ground and the Home Office spy stood over me, prodding me gently with his foot.

'We don't want you, Williamson. You will make things complicated.'

The street seemed to be filled with running men, but I seemed to lie, as it were, in a backwater, out of the current. The men who had so easily carried me from the fight stood nearby and the mob avoided us.

'It's over, Williamson. We have Michael Radford. We have Sir Charles Crawley. You've given us all we needed.' He prodded me again. 'Go away, little man. It's time you were back in Devon.'

He turned his back and walked to where I saw two constables dragging off Michael. His head lolled on his chest and his clothes were covered in his blood, but his feet stumbled under him as they pulled him along, so I knew he was alive.

Behind, on the ground, lay Harry. I raised myself to my feet and staggered towards him.

His features were almost invisible under the blood. I took his hand and reached for a pulse. There was nothing.

Harry Price was dead.

CHAPTER ELEVEN

I went back to my lodgings. What else could I have done? The police occupied the house on Queen Street. The Home Office's spies had warned me off and stayed to make sure their warning was observed. I walked back to Marylebone, a beaten man.

I let myself into the sad little room that I had called home those past weeks and lay down on my bed. I half expected a visit from the anonymous organiser of the day's events, but he did not appear. It seems that, having got what he wanted, he was indeed going to allow me to escape.

Michael, though, would not escape. And as for Harry, he had already paid the ultimate penalty.

As I lay there, I heard a clock strike twelve. Only noon and so much had happened.

I stayed in that room, staring at the ceiling, seeing nothing, until the sound of the dinner gong roused me. It was easier to go downstairs to the anonymous meat that our landlady served on a Tuesday than it was to stay abed and deal with her anxious enquiries after my health.

I had thought that there might be some talk over dinner about the events of the morning, but I had forgotten the unbridgeable chasm that separated Seven Dials from the world of civilisation. The Army could have marched in and put the place to the torch and I doubt that anyone North of Holborn would have noticed, save to complain of the smoke.

The next morning I withdrew a hundred pounds from my bank and returned to Queen Street. The place was quiet; there seemed to be fewer people around on the street and the children stood like the adults in ones and twos instead of their usual noisy groups.

I had wondered if I would find a policeman standing guard at the door, but, of course, there was none. After the events of the previous day, a single policeman could not have been expected to survive an hour on that street. Inside, I found John-John mechanically clearing the debris from the previous day's battle. I gave him the money and told him that we would bury Harry in style.

It was an unheard of sum in Seven Dials but I had no fear that it would be misappropriated. The poor take funerals seriously. I thought of all the forged five-pound notes we had distributed through funeral parlours. John-John's money would be inspected very thoroughly indeed, but the notes were good. Harry Price would be given an honest send off.

The funeral was two days later. Two plumed horses drew the coffin and John-John had distributed the money to ensure that everybody who followed the hearse had at least a black tie and a crêpe armband. The first three rows in the procession wore full mourning. It was as fine a funeral as Seven Dials would have seen that year.

When it was over, I sat with John-John at the Jolly Sandboys. It was the public house nearest to the cemetery and a regular house-of-call for mourners. There must have been around forty other funeral parties in there afternoon, but Harry's friends remarked with satisfaction that the one from Seven Dials was the largest of them all.

'Is there any news of Michael?' I asked.

John-John shook his head. 'The Peelers have him hidden away somewhere.'

'Do you have any idea where?'

Another shake of the head.

I chewed my ham sandwich. Cold ham seemed obligatory at funerals, so I had ordered sandwiches for everybody in our party. It seemed the least I could do. After all, I could afford it.

I watched the men eating with the enthusiasm of those who cannot be sure when they would next see a decent meal. Michael had given them hope and direction and, for many, the possibility of earning enough to stay alive. Now, despite the promises I had been given, he was in the hands of the police.

I had to do something, but I was at a loss to know where to start. The police seemed to be keeping Michael hidden away somewhere. The man from the Home Office had taken care that I should never learn his name. How could I argue that he should keep his promise when I didn't even know who he was? I had nowhere to start my search.

There was laughter from a corner of the room where some of the boys had gathered. They had been subdued after the fighting, but they were recovering now with the natural resilience of the young. I recognised the lads who had pointed out the Home Office spies and I had the beginnings of an idea.

I waited until we were back in Seven Dials before I approached them. This was not a conversation I wanted overheard outside that neighbourhood.

I had taken the opportunity to slip into a confectioners and I was carrying a bag of the raspberry drops that they so obviously appreciated. I held the sweets out as an opening gambit, then, as the sticky red confectionary vanished into their mouths, I asked, 'The fellows you saw spying on us here – have you ever seen them anywhere else?'

The boys said nothing for a while. Either they were concentrating on my question or they were savouring the sweets.

'While you were round and about,' I prompted. The boys got everywhere. They lived by petty thieving, mostly,

191

so there wasn't much that went on within a mile or two of Seven Dials that they did not know.

The younger lad looked pointedly at the remaining fruit drops and I offered him another. 'Might have seen the geezer with a broken nose.' A long pause. I offered him the bag again. 'He drinks at the Mitre.'

'Every night?'

Another sharp look at the bag.

'Tell me and you can have them all.'

'Near enough. Usually comes in about nine.'

I handed over the sweets and the boys were off to enjoy their prize in some secluded place where they would not be required to share. I, in my turn, was about to pay another visit to the docks.

The next night found me on Holborn with two strong men very similar to those who had accompanied me on my first visit to Seven Dials. They weren't the same two men, for ships come and go and the faces in the dockside taverns change from night to night. These two had taken a little longer to recruit, for the task they were to assist me with would put them firmly outside the law.

The Mitre is set back from the road, down a narrow, ill-lit alley. This served my purpose very well. We could wait unobserved, but with a clear view of the drinkers as they entered or left when, for a moment, their faces were illuminated by the light through the open door.

My acquaintance with the broken nose did not leave until close to midnight. It had been a long wait, but the inconvenience that had caused was more than offset by the fact that when he left, he left alone. My two lads were on him in seconds. They shoved a dirty rag into his mouth to discourage any attempt at shouting and dragged him away from the main road and further up the alley where we could reasonably expect to be left in peace for a few minutes at least.

'We're going to take the gag out,' I explained, 'and you are going to talk very, very quietly. Or scream very, very loudly. It's your choice, really. Do you understand?'

He nodded and I took out the rag.

Apparently he had decided to do the sensible thing and be quiet. I was glad, for I wanted no violence that I could avoid.

'You've been doing some work of late in Seven Dials.' He started to shake his head and I struck him. I wasn't proud of it, but when I thought of Michael imprisoned and Harry dead and the lies I had been told, I wasn't ashamed either.

I think he recognised my anger and that decided him. He admitted to the work that he had done and, more importantly, who he had done it for.

'His name is Mr Torrance.'

'And where can I find Mr Torrance?'

There was a moment's hesitation and I took out a knife I had purchased especially for this eventuality. Fortunately, I didn't have to use it.

Mr Torrance inhabited a very dull office in a very dull building just off Whitehall. I arrived at the desk early the next morning, dressed in my most respectable suit. The clerks were quite obsequious and when I presented my card and asked if it would be convenient to see Mr Torrance, I was assured that my card would be presented to him and would it be convenient for me to wait?

Mr Torrance was an unpleasant man with fixed ideas when it came to foreign plots and suchlike, but he was not a fool. He did not pretend that he was unavailable or try to fob me off with some implausible tale. Ten minutes after I arrived, I was in his room.

'You must have gone to some lengths to find me here. I do not know why, because whatever you want, I fear you will be disappointed.'

A clerk appeared, bearing his master a cup of tea. I was not offered any.

'I want Michael Radford.'

He raised his eyebrows in that supercilious way I had become so familiar with. 'What makes you think I could give you Michael Radford, even were I disposed to do so?'

'He's not been brought before the magistrates. So he's not being held by the regular police.'

'He's not a regular prisoner. He's involved in treason. Conspiring with a foreign power – or foreign powers. We haven't quite decided yet. We're making further enquiries.'

'He's not involved with anybody. He's a Devon man who came to London and fell in with bad company.'

'He fell in with Sir Charles Crawley. And Mr Marx. Traitors and anarchists and plotting against the Crown.'

'That's bosh, and you know it.'

He sipped his tea and said nothing.

'You want Sir Charles. Radford is nothing to you.'

'I have Sir Charles. I have witnesses put him at the house in Seven Dials. I have French money found in his own home, and seditious books by that Marx fellow. I have the printing press. It took a while to find it, but we did.'

'So why Michael?'

'"Michael," is it now? I understand his' – he paused as if searching for a word –'his *friend* is dead. Do you have an interest in that direction?'

For a moment, I was more than half inclined to reach across his desk and take his throat and squeeze until he was on his way to explain himself to his Maker. But I restrained myself. I would not give him the satisfaction of seeing how much his words had hurt me.

'You don't need him and you promised me that if I helped you, you would not harm him.'

'I wouldn't have pursued him had he not been there

when the police moved in. But he is scarcely under my protection.'

I had only one possibility of saving him. Everything hung up on what came next.

'If you do not release him, I will tell everyone that the currency you found in Sir Charles' house was forged.'

Torrance's face froze.

'It's no more French than I am.'

'You're lying.'

'You know I'm not.'

He stared at me for what seemed a very long time. Then slowly, regretfully, he nodded. 'No, you're not, are you?'

'And the seditious book is hardly evidence, as it? It's not illegal. Anybody can buy it.'

Torrance sat back and tried to recover his composure. 'Notes on Communist writing, translated into English, concealed in his home.'

'Left by a respectable academic gentleman, when Sir Charles was not at home. I'm sure he'll be happy to appear as a witness at any trial.'

He looked suddenly very tired. 'You were the man with a limp. None of the watchers at the house had seen you before.' He shook his head with regret. 'A foolish mistake. I must be getting old.'

I made no reply.

'If Radford is released, I will stay quiet. You can have Sir Charles.'

Torrance leaned forward, as if desperate to draw closer, to convince me that what he said next would be true. 'The man is a traitor, you know. Perhaps the French put him up to this, perhaps not. But he has betrayed his country.' He paused and shuffled some papers on his desk. 'We are not entirely foolish, Williamson. We know things. Not always things we can prove in court, but we know things.'

My experience of Mr Torrance and his men had already

convinced me of the truth of this. They might see plots where none existed or choose to believe that working men struggling for a better life must be agents of foreign power, but when it came to observing people and collecting the simple facts about them, the organisation was terrifyingly efficient.

'What will you do?'

'I don't need to do anything. If you make a nuisance of yourself, you could always have an accident.'

'I could.' I pretended a calm confidence I did not really feel. 'But I remember when we first met. You said something about the importance of discretion. "We value discretion above almost all things," I think it was. I'm a survivor of Cawnpore. I am, whatever you and I know to the contrary, accounted a gentleman. Is arranging an "accident" for me what you would account discretion?'

He steepled his fingers, as if in thought, and looked at me across the desk. There was the beginning of a smile on his face – the first glimmer of warmth I had ever seen in the man. 'I think, on reflection, that the first thing I will do is to release Mr Radford. Are you still in your lodging house?'

'I thought that now this business is concluded, I might move back to the Royal Hotel.'

The smile was broader now. 'A wise choice. And so convenient for a train to Devon. I will see that Mr Radford is conveyed to the hotel this afternoon. It would be wise if both of you were to leave the metropolis at the earliest possible opportunity.'

He rose and showed me to the door. As I was about to leave, he shook my hand. 'I wasn't sure about you, Williamson,' he said. 'All that running around in the Far East. I thought you were the sort of fellow who can lord it over the natives, but wouldn't cut it here in England. I was wrong.'

I had no idea how to respond. I just pumped my hand

up and down and smiled, and then a clerk was escorting me downstairs.

That was the end of the tale, really. Michael was delivered, safe and sound, by two more of Mr Torrance's discreetly anonymous fellows. He had been kept in a cell in a basement in one of those undistinguished official buildings that seem to have sprung up all over the centre of London. People kept asking him about Sir Charles and the French and whether or not he was a Communist. He told me that after a while he was tired and confused and simply told them the truth in the hope that they would leave him alone, but they never did. The truth, after all, was that he had come to London to make his fortune and discovered that the only way he could stay alive was to turn to crime. It was as simple as that, but that was not a story they were ever going to believe.

I took him back to Bickleigh. It wasn't what he wanted, but what choice did either of us have? Nobody had taken over his cottage and Mrs Slattery spoke up on his behalf, so he moved back in and seemed set to continue as he had all the years he lived in the village.

News of Harry's death was a nine-day wonder. Michael and I agreed we would not tell people the truth of what had happened. Michael had found him in Seven Dials and they had shared a room, working as labourers on the railway. Then Harry had been attacked on his way back from the pub one night and he had died. It was a straightforward story and there was no reason why it should not be believed.

I read the London papers for any news of the riot or the counterfeiting or any trial for treason, and there was nothing. It was as if it had never happened. Then, two weeks later, tucked away between the news of a duchess giving birth and a duke's daughter getting married, there were a few lines about the death of Sir Charles Crawley,

Baronet. He had been killed in another of those wretched accidents with a runaway horse.

I imagined Mr Torrance reading the article, sipping his tea, and allowing himself another little smile.

I bought The Grange. After my visit to London, I decided that a quiet life in the country would probably suit me better.

I visited Michael as often as I could without it appearing unseemly. He settled back into his old life and, if he seemed quieter and more withdrawn than in the past, people put that down to his London adventure having been a failure. Only with me could he talk about Harry.

I think Michael had always known my nature, as I suppose I must always have known his, though I had denied it to myself. In time, sharing our memories of Harry and the time we all spent together in that house in Queen Street, we grew closer.

I had servants at The Grange, of course. It was expected, and besides the place was too big for me to look after myself. Valuing my privacy, though, I hired girls from the village who lived out.

I seldom entertained, and, when I did, an older woman from the village – a widow with a face that discouraged any doubts as to her perfect respectability – would stay for the night, doing her best on her own once Cook had finished her tasks in the kitchen and departed. One night, Mr and Mrs Slattery were dining with me, for I never forgot his early hospitality and they were my most frequent guests. Our maid for the night, struggling to clear the second remove by herself, had dropped a plate. It was no great matter, but Slattery remarked on it later.

'You shouldn't be here on your own in the evenings, John,' he said. 'It's bad for the spirit and terribly hard on the old girl. She shouldn't be kept up of a night waiting on you.'

I agreed, but said that I had lived my life so far without keeping a woman under my roof and had no particular desire to change that now.

'Why a woman, then, John? A big place like this, you should be thinking of a man-servant.' He looked me straight in the eye as he spoke. Did he guess my secret? I will never know, but Mrs Slattery blushed and said that that was a splendid idea and what about young Radford who had seemed awfully unsettled since his adventures in London, and then she blushed again and started to talk about the weather. The hot weather had finally broken and in October a great storm has swept across the countryside. No one had ever seen anything like it, she said, and Mr Slattery nodded and blamed the railways.

'Unnatural things. Cutting through the air at speeds like that. Of course it changes the weather. We'll have worse storms in the future, you mark my words.'

And so the evening meandered on, as evenings with friends are wont to do. But afterwards I thought of what the Slatterys had said and the more I thought of it, the better the idea seemed.

It was a month or more before I made up my mind to put the idea before Michael. I had thought he might take it amiss, for he had always been suspicious of charity. 'But this won't be charity,' I explained and, rather to my surprise, he nodded and agreed.

'We have to face the facts, John. We don't belong anymore in the lives we were born into. We have to make our own lives, and I think it will be pleasant to make them together.'

The Grange is a big house. Michael has his rooms and I have mine and, though we are good friends we are, as yet, no more than that. But our home stands off from the village. If we ever want to change our domestic arrangements, that will be nobody's business but ours, whatever the law says. As time passes and the memory of Harry Price and his death fades, our friendship may still grow into love.

I was born in Bickleigh but I left and travelled the world. I have spent most of my life alone. Now I am come back to Bickleigh and God willing, I will die here. I hope that, in the years that are left me, I will not have to be alone again.

EDITOR'S NOTES

1859 was an interesting time in England. Victoria had already been on the throne for twenty-two years, but in many ways this was still the England of the early nineteenth century. In London the great slums, or rookeries, were slowly being demolished, but those that remained were a horrific reminder of an earlier age. We were only twenty years from the time of Sherlock Holmes, who bridges the Victorian and Edwardian eras, but policing and social order in 1859 was nothing like the situation in the 1880s.

London was growing massively from a city of under a million people in 1801 to almost two million in 1841. By 1861, the population (boosted by Irish immigrants fleeing the potato famine) was 2.8 million and the city was the largest in the Western world. John Williamson naturally compares the metropolis with Calcutta, a famously populous city, but in 1859 London actually had many times more inhabitants than Calcutta, which had a population of several hundred thousand in the 1850s. (For this, as for various other bits of useful historical trivia, I am grateful to my own editor, Greg Rees, who seems to have an encyclopaedic knowledge of such detail.)

It was a time of enormous social and technological change, and John Williamson found himself caught between the old eighteenth-century world and the modern world emerging from its decay.

Most of the story takes place in London, centring on Seven Dials. I'm a frequent visitor to the Seven Dials Club, so it's an area I know reasonably well.

I think the first time I came across Seven Dials in literature was in Disraeli's *Sybil*, in which the heroine is rescued from a mob there. It is depicted as a place of utter lawlessness. Reading about it in other works of fiction and non-fiction, different people seem to describe it very differently. To some, it is just a noisome slum, to others an unspeakably vile place. Williamson's version veers towards the negative, but his Seven Dials is by no means the worst you can find in literature.

It's odd looking at the town you live in, in a period not that long ago. My grandfather was a policeman in Soho, no distance from Seven Dials, less than fifty years after the time of this book. I have a picture of Victorian London made up from books written then (Dickens is brilliant for period feel), stories that have built up about the town, modern novels and, for all they're full of errors, films set in the nineteenth century.

There are a lot of books that can help you understand Williamson's London. The one I started with was *The Victorian Underworld* by Donald Thomas. It's a brilliant overview, though (like many other books) it relies rather heavily on Henry Mayhew's *London Labour and the London Poor*. Mayhew's enormous work is more than most people will ever get right through, but it's well worth dipping in and out of. I've read several accounts of coining, but Mayhew's is the best. He confirms Williamson's statements about the discounted rate for buying forged currency. He is also full of fascinating details, such as the areas most habituated by prostitutes. (Williamson's first trip out with Susan to the Burlington Arcade reflects Mayhew's opinion of that locale.) Another source of local colour is Bradshaw's *Illustrated Hand Book to London and its Environs 1862*, recently republished by Conway.

For more about coining I turned to the records of the Old Bailey. Williamson is over-optimistic about the sentence coiners might expect – looking at sentences around this time we see Thomas Ferryman (Sept 1858) receiving five years for what seems to have been an extensive amount of forgery. Richard Pike (Jan 1859) was given four years for forging shillings, while Joseph Pomeroy (Jan 1860) got ten years for forging sixpences. However, the same records suggest that convictions for coining were rare. As Michael suggested when the police raided them, it was essential for the police to find actual coining equipment to get a prosecution. It was much more common, therefore, for people to be prosecuted for possessing or passing the coins. Here, sentences were much lighter. In the summer of 1859 most of those convicted got a sentence of only a few months or one or two years, although sentences for repeat offenders were much higher. This is presumably the reason that Williamson saw it as not being a particularly serious offence.

Passing banknotes was, for all the reassurance Williamson gave to people using them to pay for funerals, taken more seriously. In 1857 William Stone got five years for passing a forged fiver, while Joseph and Thomas Collins both got ten years (although they both seemed to have been heavily involved in forgery). Forging the notes meant even longer sentences: in 1857 James Bolyne got fifteen years for forging £5 notes. Interestingly, despite this, Michael's concern about forging £10 notes was not shared by many others. Mayhew says that forged tenners were quite common.

The forging of foreign currency was also surprisingly common in London with Turkish and Russian money being produced in quantity by some forgers.

It was not unusual for juries to recommend mercy and sentences to be reduced on this account. I've seen no suggestion that the death of a child would incline juries to clemency although mercy might be recommended on lots of grounds – for example, 'being a stranger to the country' or extreme old age. Eliza Clark (May 1862) received a much reduced sentence because the jury considered her to have been 'the tool of another person'. Williamson might have believed the assurances that he was giving to bereaved parents.

Ever since I learned that Karl Marx used to cabal with his Communist comrades in Great Windmill Street, I have always hoped to read more about his life in London. Marx is as I imagined him from Francis Wheen's immensely readable biography. His concerns about money and the unfortunate Mr Biskamp are reflected in his published correspondence with Engels.

A nice overview of this time and place is provided by Liza Picard's *Victorian London*.

For more about life on the farm in Devon, you can read Henry Stephens' *Book of the Farm*. This excellent work would have enabled anybody at the time to establish a model farm and Mr Slattery was obviously guided by its precepts.

Like any Englishman, Williamson frequently comments on the weather and its unnatural warmth. The summer of 1859 was, indeed, unusually hot and dry, the weather finally breaking in the great storm that he mentions in October.

T.W.

THE WILLIAMSON PAPERS

TOM WILLIAMS

For more information about **Tom Williams**

and other **Accent Press** titles

please visit

www.accentpress.co.uk

Lightning Source UK Ltd.
Milton Keynes UK
UKOW01f2244060416